"I've com[e]
to have an affair."

"Indeed," Marc murmured. "Many men come here for the same purpose. Don't make yourself too available."

Megan felt properly reprimanded. "That's my bungalow," she said shortly. "Good night."

"Oh, Megan. There is just one more thing...."

Marc kissed her with the expertise of an accomplished lover. Masterfully, he drew her into a tentative response. Then, as quickly as it had begun, it was over.

"For good luck on your new venture," he said, smiling. "I'm not applying for the position, you understand. I'm not quite ready for a femme fatale such as yourself."

Megan gasped in rage. "You—you were making fun of me! You—"

"Monster?" he supplied helpfully. "There are a lot of them out there Megan," he called after her as she slammed the door.

A Modern Girl

Rebecca Flanders

Harlequin Books

TORONTO • NEW YORK • LONDON
AMSTERDAM • PARIS • SYDNEY • HAMBURG
STOCKHOLM • ATHENS • TOKYO • MILAN

Original hardcover edition published in 1983
by Mills & Boon Limited

ISBN 0-373-02623-4

Harlequin Romance first edition June 1984

CHAPTER ONE

'HOLD it, darling!'

Although Megan knew no one who would be calling her 'darling' this far from home, she had thought herself to be alone on the beach and it was instinct to turn toward the sound of the voice. As she did a man leapt down from the sandy embankment and landed not three feet in front of her, causing her to gasp and take an unplanned step backwards. He was wearing brief red swimming trunks and an open printed shirt—the usual tourist garb—and he had an expensive-looking camera about his neck, the shutter of which he was clicking rapidly.

'What are you doing?' she cried. 'You can't——'

'Marvellous, marvellous!' he exclaimed, never once taking his eyes from the view-finder. He spoke rapidly and musically, his accent curiously Continental. 'What is this—are you angry? No, perhaps more startled, and—yes, just a little worried now, for here is this fiend after you with a camera and you don't quite know what to think . . . that's it, that's it . . . Turn your face a little . . . Look at what that sun does to your eyes! I love it!'

She was backing up slowly, he was following her. The warm tide nipped at her bare feet and the early morning breeze whipped her voile cover-up about her bikini-clad body. She stammered, more than a little alarmed, 'N-now, you just wait a minute ... stay away from me ...'

'But you know I won't,' he intoned hypnotically, never once looking up. 'You know I can't resist you—what man could resist you—and your power frightens you a little, doesn't it? What is it you are running from—me, or yourself? Ah, those eyes! A myriad emotions in those eyes! Is that wanting I see?'

'It certainly is not!' she exclaimed, still backing away. 'And if you don't go away and leave me alone I'll scream—I swear I will!'

'Lovely! Scream by all means, but it will make little difference, for in the end I'll have you, and you know that, don't you?'

She gasped, and he continued, 'Ah, vain protests! Ah, foolish flight! Soon shall we see a virgin's tears? She has come seeking adventure, but the adventure has found her too soon, and is she frightened by what she cannot control?'

That was uncanny. Now she was really frightened. She turned to make a more effective flight, but the shifting sand beneath her feet caught her off balance. She landed with a cry in the miry sand, the incoming tide rushing about her waist.

He was on his knees before her, laughing now as he splashed water in her face, never once glancing up from the camera as he continued to work the shutter. Megan did try to scream as she made a weak, unco-ordinated defence of herself, but it came out as more of a gasping squeak. Sea-water soaked her hair and splashed in her mouth and stung her eyes.

And then he announced abruptly, 'That's it.' He stood and extended his hand to help her up, but she only sat there, gaping at him.

For the first time, she got a good look at her tormentor. He was tall, and seemed even taller from her position on the ground while he towered above her. His legs were firm and well-muscled, and his stance emphasised hard, rounded calves and sinewy thighs which might have belonged to a runner. His waist was trim and his chest broad, covered with a mat of dark hair that gleamed with a reddish tint in the sunlight in a triangular shape which extended upward from the navel. His tan was light and even, he had somehow avoided the rakish, pirate look most dark men get when they tan. There was a startling red streak running through his jet-black hair—Megan had never seen *anything* like that, and she was unwillingly fascinated even while part of her mind registered vengefully that that peculiarity would make him much easier to describe to the police. His eyes, set off by the golden tan of his face, were a sparkling, crystal blue.

She sat there, water dripping from her curls on to her cheekbones and her eyelashes, and said in a tiny, wondering voice, 'You're crazy.'

He grinned and bent down to grasp her arm, pulling her to her feet. 'So I've been told,' he agreed. 'Now, you appear to be unharmed, except for your clothes, of course. I'll pay for the damage, naturally.' He broke off his rapid dialogue to reach out and touch her dripping, yellow-white curls lightly. 'Gorgeous hair,' he murmured. Then, in his usual clipped, hurried tones, 'It will dry as good as new. I wish my girls were that practical. Sorry I don't have my wallet with me, love,' he added in a rush as he turned to go, 'you'll have to stop by the hotel later and my secretary will give you a cheque. *Ciao* for now, pet!'

Megan simply stared after him as he made a quick escape, jogging down the beach. Just before he disappeared behind a sand dune he turned and lifted his hand to her, grinning. The breeze whipped his dark hair over his eyes and there was a dimple on the left side of his chin which gave his face an endearing, disarmingly youthful look. She had to frown in puzzlement and alarm to keep herself from returning that contagious grin.

Well, she thought as she brushed the damp sand off the back of her legs and wrung out the hem of her wrapper, that's *one* way to start a vacation!

In fact, had she not been so preoccupied and still a little shaken by the episode, she would have admitted there could not have been a more perfect way to start this particular vacation. After all, wasn't that exactly what she had come for? For once in her life, she wanted to do something daring, actively seek new experiences, adventure, and—yes, romance. And Bermuda seemed the perfect place to begin such a quest.

In actual fact, Megan was breaking away. She was tired of her dull staid life, the days spent working as a receptionist in her home town's one medical clinic, the evenings spent watching television at home with her parents or going out on very uninspired dates with George, the home-town boy everyone assumed she would marry. She was tired of getting brittle, exciting letters from former college friends describing their sophisticated lives and their multitude of lovers, and tired of having nothing to write in reply.

It was not that she disliked her job—in fact, she found it very fulfilling—and of course she loved her parents. She simply felt at times that life had passed her by; she was a twentieth-century girl living a Victorian life, and she had made up her mind to do something about it.

The trip to Bermuda was the perfect beginning. Here she was not sweet, reliable, perfectly conventional Megan Brown, who had not missed a day of work in three years and who still lived at home like a proper unmarried girl should. Here she was sophisticated, mysterious, adventurous, provocative . . . and eager for romance.

Although Megan considered herself a very ordinary-looking girl she received her share of admiring glances from early-morning male bathers as she made her way back to her bungalow to change. She was small-framed and not very tall, but her figure was so well proportioned that she could wear a bikini without trepidation. She was naturally slim and rarely worried about her weight, for which reason she was the envy of many of her girl friends. For this trip, she had clipped her naturally curly blonde hair just below the ears, hoping for a more sophisticated, modern look. She was not displeased with the result. The soft, baby-fine curls framed her small, heart-shaped face much more attractively than the long pony-tail had done, and emphasised her wide, startlingly green eyes.

But she touched her still-damp curls with a small frown as she let herself inside the bungalow. *He* had said her hair-style was practical. She did not want to be practical.

However, it was convenient to be able to shower the salt water from her hair and simply towel it dry, ready to pick up her day where it had left off without the fuss of blow-driers or curlers. She changed into a pair of snug white ducks and a red checked tie-top for breakfast, and walked over to the hotel.

Sometimes she regretted her decision to rent a private bungalow for the duration of her two-week stay. After all, if the purpose of her vacation had been to meet people (*men*, she had to admit honestly to herself, vital, attractive romantic men who were the farthest thing imaginable from the dull, presentable, perfectly correct men she was used to), then wouldn't she have fared better at the hotel? Perhaps her penchant for privacy was a left-over from the past she had decided to cut, and it was a hard habit to break.

Immediately as she walked into the busy, colourful hotel dining room, she remembered. He had said *he* was staying here. In that case, she reflected wryly, perhaps she was better off staying as far away from the hotel as possible.

She tried not to think too much about that encounter on the beach this morning, because it brought back too clearly George's appalled look and her father's stern warnings when she had announced her intention to take this vacation alone. No doubt there *were* dangers in travelling alone, and possibly a single girl *was* prey to every lecher and unscrupulous wolf on the beach, but one could hardly go through life avoiding every element of danger without avoiding also some of life's richest adventures. And besides, no harm had actually been done. And he *did* have the most endearing grin . . .

The buffet featured a selection of dishes, from the standard bacon and eggs to the kidneys and kippers that were common in this predominantly British island, to the lush tropical fruits and fluffy breads of native origin. Feeling exotic, Megan selected a thick slice of pineapple, a wedge of papaya, and half a melon she couldn't identify.

From behind her a curiously familiar voice said, 'You can't possibly eat all that, my dear—where would you put it?'

She turned and gasped, 'You!'

He gave her another one of his devastating grins. 'In the flesh.' He reached around her to fill his cup with steaming tea, and she automatically shrank back a little as his arm brushed against her shoulder. 'You seem to have recovered quite nicely,' he continued, touching her back lightly to urge her through the queue. 'Have you been up to my suite yet?'

She stared at him, astounded, and then realised he could not possibly have meant that the way it sounded. She remembered his offer to pay for her damaged clothes and murmured, 'No, really, it's not necessary——'

But he was saying, 'Come now, you don't want anything else to eat, do you? No, I think that will quite do.' His hand was firmly on her back now, and steering her away from the buffet. 'I've just time for one more cup, and you can keep me company. Devilish schedule, this, but fortunately I'm a morning person—as I would say you are too from what I know of you . . .'

Megan stared at him as he took her plate from her and deposited it on the table, then said wonderingly, 'It's amazing.'

He pulled out her chair. 'What is, lovely?'

'The way you have of carrying on a conversation completely by yourself.'

He did not look in the least abashed. The bright blue eyes twinkled. 'A professional hazard, I suppose. But it is rather exhausting, so I'll tell you what . . . you talk while I drink my tea in leisure.'

She looked around the dining room uneasily. It was crowded with tourists, all involved in their separate meals and conversations, and surely no harm could come to her here—even if she did dine with a crazy person. Still, she resented his overbearing manner on principle, and she objected, 'I didn't invite you to sit with me.'

'No, of course not, I invited *you*. Now, do take your seat, dear, you're blocking traffic.'

She sat down in exasperation. 'Do you make a habit of this?' she demanded. 'Accosting strange women and bending them to your will?'

'Hardly ever,' he assured her with a wink, and sat down across from her. 'As a matter of fact, I can't recall meeting a strange woman in my life, much less accosting one. And what about you? Are you in the habit of letting yourself be picked up by strange men?'

Humour sparkled in his eyes, and it was contagious. 'Hardly ever,' she replied drily, and cut herself a small piece of pineapple. After all, he appeared to be perfectly harmless now—although a bit eccentric in a deep pink shirt which appeared to be silk, worn over jeans and leather sandals— and she was not about to make a scene in this crowded dining room.

He said, smiling, 'Marvellous.' Although she was not certain whether that comment was a reflection on her reply, or life in general. She kept her attention on her plate, and was surprised by the silence which followed, disturbed only by the clatter of background noises—chatting diners and the clink of cutlery.

When she ventured a glance at him, she discovered he was simply gazing at her, his chin resting on his hand as he sipped his tea, and in his eyes was the soft light of appreciation which comes only from a man who knows women intimately and loves everything he knows. It was an intense, studying, memorising look, categorising each new discovery he made in her face with a new expression of wonder in those bright blue eyes, and Megan felt herself begin to blush. She was unused to such scrutiny, especially from a man such as this . . . vital, attractive, wordly-wise. Just as she was beginning to seriously consider changing her table, he murmured, as though in a half-reverie. 'Delightful. Utterly delightful.' Then, abruptly, 'Well, then, I'm waiting. You were going to tell me the story of your perfectly charming little life in sixty seconds or less, because I'm afraid, my dear, that's all I have to spare.'

She stared at him incredulously. 'You *are* crazy!'

'I believe we've already established that,' he replied equitably. 'Now let me see if I can speed this up a little, for time, as they say, is of the essence . . . You're from the States, obviously, just over for a little holiday, arrived last evening or very early this morning, you have a nice young man waiting back home, you're a secretary or a receptionist, and your age is . . .' he hesitated a moment. 'Approximately twenty-three. So far so good?'

Megan's eyes widened. 'How in the world——?'

But his eyes only twinkled as he lifted a finger to silence her. 'That's my business, my dear. Shall I go on?'

'No!' she exclaimed, totally at a loss.

'It's just as well,' he replied, glancing at his watch. 'I have to rush off. Do be a smart girl, now, and be careful of the sun today,' he added, patting her shoulder as he passed. 'You wouldn't want to end up with a nasty burn.'

She could only stare after him, speechless and amazed, as he disappeared into the crowd near the lobby like a phantom.

It was all very exciting, really, and it was impossible to concentrate on her breakfast. The adventure had begun more promisingly than she had dared imagine, despite the fact that she would probably never see that particular fascinating man again—she didn't even know his name!—but her eagerness increased for the coming day. She signalled the waitress for her check.

'Oh, Mr Campion has already taken care of it, miss,' the pretty dark-skinned girl told her with a smile.

She looked at her in confusion. 'Mr—Campion?'

'Yes, ma'am, the photographer.'

Photographer! So he wasn't crazy after all, just an eccentric British photographer—that explained a lot. 'Do you mean,' she clarified, 'the man who was sitting here . . .'

'Yes, ma'am.' The girl gave a little giggle. 'He and his girls have kept the place in an uproar this past week, I can tell you that, but he does seem very charming, doesn't he?'

'Yes,' agreed Megan absently, 'he does.' His *girls*?

'Will there be anything else, ma'am?'

'No, thank you,' she answered as she rose.

'Have a nice day, ma'am.'

Megan replied that she intended to.

She left the hotel wondering whether Mr Campion travelled with his own private harem, or whether that, too, was merely a 'professional hazard.'

CHAPTER TWO

SHE tried to put him out of her mind as she went about her souvenir shopping that morning, except to hope that the chance encounter with such a totally improbable stranger was a good portent for what the rest of her vacation would hold.

She had wanted to get the shopping out of the way on her first day, for she had promised everyone some little trinket as a memento of her trip. But the colourful little shops with their quaint stone roofs and exotically scented interiors intrigued her, and she spent much more time selecting her purchases than she had intended. For her mother she bought a brightly printed silk scarf, for her father a meerschaum pipe, for Dr Brandon a coral paperweight (after all, it had been greatly through his generosity with Christmas bonuses over the years that she had been able to afford this trip, and she could not exclude him from her list) and for the girls in the office she bought a selection of pretty polished shell necklaces and bracelets. George presented something of a problem, but she finally decided on a handsomely bound book dealing with the history of the islands which he would consider both tasteful and practical.

But for herself she was not at all practical. She selected a perfume blended of tropical flowers whose scent was sensuous and mysterious and unlike anything she had ever worn before. There was a pair of coral combs studded with tiny green stones which, for the price, she hoped were emeralds. She bought a luxuriously romantic shawl of hand-woven lace, then had to force herself to stop browsing before she ran short of funds.

She chose to walk the smooth stone streets which led past the hotel and toward the beach, delighting in the colourful horse-drawn carriages and the native bicyclers who were her companions. It was long after noon when she arrived at her bungalow, and she decided to skip lunch in favour of sunning on the beach.

There was a group of about a dozen of the charming, mock-thatched cabins set back from the beach, and most, she was to discover, were rented to families. On one side of her was a middle-aged couple with two noisy children, on the other three young girls with long, sunbleached hair and perfect tans. They were supervised by a stern older woman who could have been an aunt. She had not exactly chosen the swinging singles area in which to spend her vacation.

On the beach it was much of the same. Children splashed in the tide and played leapfrog over sand-castles, watched by indulgent mothers at a distance. The occasional winks and admiring glances Megan got as she spread her towel on the sand were from middle-aged men whose wives were dozing next to them, and she felt conspicuous and embarrassed in her tiny yellow print bikini. She lay on her stomach and let the warm sun beat down on her shoulders, and tried not to think of the vibrant, fascinating Mr Campion.

After a time, however, she could not help thinking of him. The sun was making her drowsy, and she remembered very clearly his warning about sunburn. Afraid of falling asleep and totally ruining her vacation with third degree burns, she reluctantly gathered up her things and went back inside. There the sun and the excitement which had robbed her of sleep the night before completely took its toll on her, and she slept deeply and dreamlessly until after sundown.

When she awoke she was angry at herself for having wasted almost an entire day napping, but she felt refreshed and eager for what the evening held in store. She dressed carefully in a pale green and white printed voile dress whose neckline was deeper than she was accustomed to—she found herself pulling at the bodice in an attempt to decently cover the soft swell of her breasts before she chided herself impatiently for being a prude. After all, she was a modern girl now, and she would dress the part. She pulled back her curls with the coral combs, and the effect was exactly what she had hoped for—up-to-date, fashionable, thoroughly sophisticated. Her sun-blushed face needed little make-up, but she applied a thin line of white liner to her eyelids and darkened the lashes with a brush of mascara. Her eyes looked enormous, and sparkled like the emeralds in her combs. The finishing touch was a pale apricot lipstick, and then just a hint of her extravagant new perfume. Why, she thought in delight and amazement as she looked at herself in the mirror, George wouldn't know me now!

She was late to dine, and the hotel dining room was subdued and not very crowded. Mostly couples sat at the occupied tables, holding hands or talking softly or simply looking adoringly into one another's eyes. She somehow found the sight vaguely depressing. Everything is made for two, she thought. And Mr Campion was not among the diners.

The menu set before her looked sumptuously inviting, but somehow she found it difficult to imagine herself enjoying a succulent prime rib or elegant lobster Thermidor by herself, and that only brought back what George had said. 'What will you *do* with yourself for two weeks all alone?' he had demanded incredulously. 'What fun can it possibly be?' Poor George, she had thought at the time, was totally lacking in the imagination it took to discern what fun a girl could devise for herself with two weeks of unrestricted freedom in the romantic islands. Now she began to wonder whether he might not have been closer to the truth than she suspected.

With a sigh, she ordered a dinner salad and let her eyes roam absently about the candlelit room. Couples were beginning to wander off now, probably to dance in the Sea Winds Lounge or walk hand in hand on the beach, and when the evening ended they would not be going to bed alone. Megan sighed again.

George had objected to the extravagance of the trip. 'It's not as though I ever waste my savings on frivolous things,' he complained. 'You know that with interest rates the way they are today you can't expect to buy a house without a substantial down payment and . . .'

That was when she made up her mind. Why, he was talking as though they were already married, and they weren't even engaged! She got a vision of what life would be like with George, plodding day in and day out in the same old circle, going to work, coming home, fixing dinner, watching television . . . making sure his meals were served exactly the way he liked them, his shirts freshly pressed, his chequebook never overdrawn . . . And she was appalled. That was when she made up her mind that when she returned from this vacation, a changed woman, she would get an apartment of her own, go to singles bars if she felt like it, dance until dawn if she felt like it and make it clear to George that she was no longer accountable to him, and that perhaps he had better start shopping around for another wife-candidate.

Of course, the way things were going, she was getting a slow start on becoming a changed woman, but after all, this was only her first full day here. The island was teeming with excitement and romance, and the air was rich with possibilities. She had only just begun.

She left the dining room and was undecided whether to linger at the hotel or do what she really wanted to do—walk on the beach in the moonlight. Perhaps it was her inborn prejudice about going anywhere unescorted, or perhaps it was simply the lure of the rich blue night and the fragrant tropical air, but she found herself leaving the bright lights of the hotel behind as she walked along the coral sea-break overlooking the beach.

At first she was not alone. Couples strolled and cuddled and murmured to one another beneath the star-studded sky, oblivious to all but themselves. A stocky old man walking his dog nodded to her curtly as he passed. She walked alone, but the rushing whisper of the surf mesmerised her, the moon was so large it seemed to fill half the sky with its muted yellow glow, and when she tipped her head back to the salty taste of the breeze the endless pattern of glittering stars made her feel dizzy and breathlessly free. She did not realise how far she had walked until she became aware of the silence. No one's footsteps crackled on the shell path but her own, even the muted sounds of music coming from the hotel and from the private cabanas along the way had faded, and here the island was as it had been from the beginning of time—uninhabited, lush with primitive beauty, and rich with promise.

But she was not quite alone. At first she thought her eyes were deceiving her, for it was quite incredible that she should accidentally encounter him again this far from all signs of civilisation. But the moonlight was bright enough to reflect the unmistakable red streak in his hair and the strong, smooth profile as he strolled along the water's edge, casually tossing shells into the surf. He was wearing a white dinner jacket, unbuttoned, and he had removed his shoes and knotted the strings together over his shoulder, to walk barefoot in the sand. His immaculately tailored dark trousers were already wet to the calves.

On an impulse, she started to call out to him, for he was walking in the opposite direction and a few feet below her, but then she had a horrible thought. They *were* awfully far from anything, and she had no real excuse for being here. Suppose he thought she had followed him? Was she really ready to behave *that* aggressively?

She didn't think so, but in the next moment the decision was made for her. She felt the narrow ledge of sand and shell begin to shift beneath her feet, then give way entirely. With a cry, she slid down the sandy embankment, to land almost directly at his feet.

For a moment he looked startled, but recovered himself quickly. He leaned over to grasp her firmly under the arms and drew her to her feet, commenting, 'It seems to be my destiny to be eternally picking you up out of the sea. Are you quite all right?'

Megan could not recall ever having been quite so embarrassed in her life, her face burned and she was grateful for the moonlight that hid her scarlet flush as she began to busily brush the sand off her legs and wring out the hem of her dress. She could do nothing but stammer incoherently, and he came to her rescue by supplying, 'Don't concern yourself. I understand I have that general effect on women.'

She looked at him, and in a moment they both burst into laughter. It was an utterly ridiculous situation, and he looked no better than she in his disarrayed dinner attire, bare feet, and wet trousers. Perhaps it was part of the magic of the islands, the ability to take nothing too seriously, to relax and let laughter come easily.

She insisted through her giggles, 'I'm really not clumsy, not usually——'

'I believe it,' he assured her. 'With a figure as lithe and petite as yours, it would be one of nature's great mistakes to strike you with clumsiness. I do hope that dress isn't ruined,' he added. 'It's quite becoming.'

'Oh, no,' she replied, 'just a little damp around the edges.' And only a short while ago she had been feeling sorry for herself because she had got all dressed up and there was no one to appreciate it. She glanced at him. 'What are you doing way out here, anyway, dressed like that?'

He gestured vaguely behind him as they began walking again, 'I just escaped from a party—dreadfully dull stuff.' His eyes were watching her with bright interest. 'And yourself?'

'Just walking,' she answered. 'I suppose I went farther than I realised. I can't even see the hotel.'

'This direction.' He caught her arm and guided her around, although she had not said she wanted to go back there. 'Are you staying there? I don't recall seeing you after our brief breakfast together.'

'No, I have a private bungalow.'

'Travelling alone?'

'That's right.'

'Well, shall we pick up the conversation where we left off at breakfast? You were telling me the story of your life.'

She laughed. 'I was doing nothing of the kind! I don't even know you.'

'Ah,' he observed softly, 'but you would like to.' The moonlight reflected on the incoming tide caught in his eye and sparked for a moment like a lively jewel. 'And that's as good a place as any to begin, I suppose. My name is Marc Campion, famed in story and song for the exquisite photos I produce for many a high-paying, glossy magazine Stateside and elsewhere ... perhaps you've seen my credit line?'

'No,' she admitted, 'I'm afraid not.'

'Peasant!' he scoffed goodnaturedly, and she laughed. He continued, 'I hail from a little town called Dunedin, New Zealand, the only son of frightfully adoring parents who, by the way, have never recovered from their disappointment over the fact that I didn't become a brain surgeon, and I'm here in Bermuda doing a brief spread on a new swimsuit collection, which just about brings us up to date. Now your turn.'

She giggled. 'Well, I don't quite know where to begin . . .'

'Let me help,' he prompted. 'What's your name?'

'Its Megan,' she told him. 'Megan Brown.'

He stopped and looked at her for a moment, the gentle, appreciative light in his eyes she remembered from the morning. 'Ah,' he said softly, 'Megan. What a dear, old-fashioned name. And how it suits you!'

She turned away from his gaze and started walking again, annoyed. Old-fashioned indeed! That was the one thing she was determined not to be.

'And so,' he continued airily, matching her stride easily, 'why has the dear, old-fashioned Megan Brown come to Bermuda, the land of romance and enchantment?'

She hesitated, and then a small, secret smile tightened her lips. She decided to throw caution to the wind. 'I've come here,' she told him, 'to have an affair.'

If an expression crossed his face the filtering moonlight hid it, and he did not reveal it by altered tone or inflection. 'Is that a fact?' he replied casually. 'Might one ask why?'

An answer to that one did not come quite so blithely, and all she could think of was, 'Well, I'm over twenty-one . . .'

'And you've never . . .?' He glanced at her, leaving the enquiry unfinished.

'I come from a small town,' she admitted, and was already beginning to regret having spoken.

He muttered, 'I see.' Then, 'and what does the small-town boy you've left behind think of all this?'

She waved it away. 'Oh, George—all he thinks about is a house in the suburbs with two cars and the proper two-point-two children per average American family. He wouldn't understand.'

'And you're not interested in this house in the suburbs and two cars and—did you say *two-point-two* children?'

'A modern woman doesn't *have* to be married,' she replied, warming to a favourite subject. 'Those times are past. After all, I'm self-sufficient, self-supporting, and there's no law that says I have to regulate my life to a man's. Women are much freer today,' she added confidently.

'Indeed,' Marc Campion murmured noncommittally, and Megan experienced a slight disappointment, fearing her outspoken manner had put him off. But then she gave an unconscious toss of her head and decided it did not matter. There was no room for chauvinism in her philosophy, and what else could she expect from a man who was used to regarding women as no more than clothes horses?

They walked in silence for a time, only the crashing of the surf against the coral reef disturbing the velvety night. At last they stood where the glittering lights of the hotel were reflected in the slippery sand, and she turned to him. 'Well, I suppose this is where we part company,' she said pleasantly. 'It was nice talking with you.'

But he touched her elbow lightly and said, 'I'll walk you back to your bungalow. You really shouldn't wander about at night unescorted, you know—no matter how independent and self-sufficient you are.'

The slight patronising tone to his words irritated her, and she tossed her head again defiantly. 'That's a very narrow-minded statement,' she retorted. '*You* wander about at night unescorted and no one thinks anything about it. What's the difference?'

'Only,' he replied mildly, his hand warm on her elbow, 'that I have about six inches and eighty pounds on you and lack the gentle dips and curves which you so charmingly possess which are likely to excite uncontrollable urges in the breasts of less than gentlemanly types.'

Megan frowned. 'That's an age-old excuse. It's all physical.'

'But that's what men and women are all about, if I'm not mistaken,' he interrupted with a patient, annoying gleam of humour. 'Physical differences!'

'Well, I'll have you know,' she replied heatedly, 'that recent studies disprove the old wives' tale about women being the weaker sex!'

He sighed in exaggerated long suffering. 'Spare me old wives' tales and statistics! Merely take my advice and don't wander about the island unescorted at night. It may surprise you to know that a great many men have come here for the same purpose you have, and you don't want to make yourself too available. Use a little discretion.'

Megan felt as though she had been properly reprimanded, and she fumbled in irritation through her evening bag for her key. 'That's my bungalow,' she said shortly, then turned to him. 'Goodnight.'

'Oh, Megan . . .' His light clasp on her arm drew her back as she started to move away. 'There is just one more thing . . .'

Marc enfolded her in his arms and lowered his face to hers before she had time to do more than take a breath. She thought in a moment of wild excitement, Is this it, then? Will it be tonight—with this fascinating, incredibly virile man? But with that excitement was a fluttering of trepidation, for it was all happening so fast, and then she had no more time for thoughts of any kind as his lips clasped hers warmly.

He kissed her with the expertise of an accomplished lover, moulding her to his strong, masculine shape with hands that were firm but gentle on her back and waist and travelled slowly up her spine towards her neck and shoulders, warm and insistent beneath her hair. A rush of adrenalin exploded her senses to titillating life as his lips drew response from hers, a swift hot flush of dizziness and an uncontrollable pounding of her heart. She had never been kissed like that before. Marc Campion left her too weak almost to respond, she could not lift her arms within his masterful embrace, although she longed for the feel of his muscular shoulders beneath her hands, she wanted to run her fingers through that smooth dark hair ... He parted her lips with his and began to gently explore the sensitive inner flesh and the even white pearls of her teeth until her resistance washed away in a gush of emotion like none she had ever experienced, one that left her weak and helpless, a vessel eager to receive him. Delicately, he drew her into a tentative response, and then, as quickly as it had begun, it was over. He kissed her lips lightly, then lifted his face, taking her face gently in both hands and tipping it upward to look at him.

'For good luck on your new venture,' he smiled. 'Will that do for a start?'

Megan's breath was coming rapidly and a little unsteadily, and a prickly chill had broken out on her arms. Her heart was still thudding in her ears and she was incapable of response, but she thought helplessly, 'Yes ... oh, yes ...!'

As though seeing the effect he had on her amused him, Marc touched her nose lightly and said, 'I'm not applying for the position, you understand, I merely wanted you to have a taste of what you were getting into. I'm afraid I'm not quite ready to be worked over by a femme fatale such as yourself.'

Megan gasped in rage and insult, the beautiful warm feelings that still tingled in her body dissolving like the fragments of a crystal sugar coating in rain. And the effect the pompous, mocking undertones his statement had on her was exactly that—like a drenching with a cold shower. 'You——!' she cried, twisting away. She could not think of anything bad enough to call him. Her eyes were snapping and her hands were shaking as she fumbled again for her key. 'You—you were making fun of me! You . . . you——'

'Monster?' he supplied helpfully. 'Cad? Beast?'

She stormed to the door and inserted the key furiously into the lock. It took three tries.

'There are a lot of them out there, Megan,' he called after her.

She slammed the door.

But Marc Campion waited until he heard the bolt catch on the other side. She knew because when she went to draw the shade he was still standing there. When he saw her, he lifted his hand lightly to her, winked, and strolled casually down the beach towards his hotel.

CHAPTER THREE

MEGAN was sunning on the beach next morning when she felt a shadow fall over her. She opened her eyes just as Marc Campion dropped to the towel beside her. 'Any luck?' he enquired lightly.

She scowled and pulled her sombrero over her face.

'Come now, poppet, you're not holding my little object lesson of last night against me, are you?' he crooned in that maddeningly musical accent. 'I only had your best interests at heart, as surely you must know. Come along, let me see that enchanting little face of yours.' He lifted the corner of her hat. 'Give us a smile.'

Megan scowled. 'If you're not buying,' she said coldly, 'don't handle the merchandise.' She pulled her hat deliberately back over her face.

He burst into a delighted roar of laughter, and curious heads turned. 'I love it!' he exclaimed. 'My dear, you're priceless! Do say you forgive me now, because I have an enormous favour to ask of you, and I don't want to start out with bad feelings.'

She lifted the edge of her hat cautiously, her expression still severe. 'What favour?'

'Forgive first,' he teased, and she let the hat drop into place again.

He gave an exaggerated sigh. 'Ah well, then, I suppose I shall just have to seduce you into compliance. Turn over.'

She flung the hat away from her face, staring at him. *'What?'*

'You're getting too much sun on your front,' he explained blandly. 'Turn over.'

She stared at him for a moment longer, then shook her head helplessly. 'You really are incredible!' she said ruefully. And it was impossible to stay angry with him, impossible to resist his charm—as he most likely knew very well.

'Why, thank you,' he replied mildly. 'You're rather incredible yourself.'

Megan was not at all sure that was a compliment, but after a moment she slowly turned over on her stomach. 'I still don't forgive you,' she mumbled.

'I'm working on it,' he replied, and squeezed some suntan oil into his palm, rubbing it between his hands for a moment before applying it to her shoulders with firm, gentle circular motions. 'What beautiful skin you have! It's a wonder it doesn't freckle. Still, you should be careful of too much sun. It will make you old and wrinkled before your time, and that would be a very great pity. There, is that nice? Do you feel all your tension and anger melting away beneath the gentle ministrations of my magic fingers?'

She smothered a giggle in the towel. But it was true. The smooth, rhythmic massage of his fingers was working a subtle magic on all her senses, around her shoulders and her upper arms, pressing and releasing, stroking and moulding ... now deftly unfastening the catch of her swimsuit and dribbling more warm oil on to the centre of her back and melting into the firm, glissading motions of his hands, now travelling to the small of her back and below, over her hips to just where the top of her bikini came, now upward again, his fingers brushing against her breasts . . . She caught her breath. That terrible pounding of her heart had begun again.

Teasing her, Marc refastened her top and poured more oil into his hands. He began working on her legs, rotating the ankles with the experienced art of a masseur, caressing and kneading her calves, moving upward to her thighs . . .

Megan sat up. 'All right,' she said a little breathlessly, hoping he would attribute her high colour to the effects of the sun, 'I forgive you. What is your favour?'

He smiled lazily, 'Ah, poppet, you forgive too easily. You must learn to be less free with your favours.' Then, leaning close, so that his crystal blue eyes fastened on hers with a mesmerising power, 'What I desire, angel face, is something that will cost you nothing, but is perhaps your most valuable possession, so rest assured I don't ask lightly . . .' He ran one finger slowly around the angle of her jaw, and finished softly. 'It's your time. I want you to pose for me.'

With difficulty, Megan broke away from his hypnotic eyes and the sincere, soothing power of his voice. It was obviously a part he enjoyed playing, and he played it so well she imagined many an impressionable young girl had been taken in . . . until they saw that mischievous twinkle in his eyes which suggested that, for him, the punch line would always be in watching how easily the women succumbed to his 'magic'. She wondered uneasily what would happen if one time he decided to disguise that revealing twinkle that called off the game, and how easily it would be to be hurt by such an expert charmer who played his part to perfection . . . if, just once, he cruelly went too far.

Then she gathered her thoughts about her and tried to make certain she had heard him correctly. 'Pose for you?' she repeated. 'Me?'

'But certainly, lovey, you.'

'But,' she floundered, 'but—don't you have models for that? I'm not exactly the haute couture type, you know.'

'Which is very fortunate, because I do have scores of models who are *very* haute couture. Perhaps that's precisely why I find you so appealing.' He was beginning it again, lightly turning her face towards the sun with his thumb and forefinger, studying the effect worshipfully. 'There is a quality you have, my dear, which is indefinable outside the lens of the camera . . . a freshness, and sincerity, an openness, a hint of wonder which takes in all of life and reflects it back as a fairy-tale . . . A warmth, rich with promise of the woman you will one day become . . .' He dropped his hand. 'Will you do it?' he demanded.

A slight frown creased her light brows. 'What do you mean—the woman I'll one day become?' she demanded in return. 'I'll have you know——'

'Please,' he groaned, 'a simple yes or no without the raving feminist lectures! I'm certain I'll get quite enough of them once were under way.'

Megan looked at him, her frown deepening into

a not unattractive pout. 'I haven't said I'd do it yet,' she mumbled. 'And I'm not sure I like the idea of—posing for you. It sounds rather sexist to me.'

Marc's lazy grin raked her up and down, and had the effect of completely disarming her—just as it was meant to. 'Oh, it is, my dear,' he assured her. 'Believe me, it is.'

'I don't approve,' she felt compelled to insist, although she knew her decision was already made, 'of women who exploit their bodies—or of men who do it for them. I——'

'My dear girl,' he exclaimed impatiently, 'what do you think this is—some over-priced behind-the-counter pin-up rag? I told you, I only work with the finest and most highly respected publications, and my girls, far from being exploited—at a hundred dollars an hour!—are in fact immortalised for ever by my art. However, if you feel——'

This time she interrupted him, her eyes wide. 'Did you say—a hundred dollars *an hour*?'

Marc lay back on his elbows, the lazy smile sparking in his eyes. 'Aha, do I see dollar signs in those greedy little eyes? How much trouble I could have saved myself all these years if I had but known the quickest way to a woman's heart is through her pocketbook!'

Megan flushed, and dropped her eyes. 'I didn't mean ... that is, I know I'm not a professional ...'

'You'll be adequately recompensed for your time, I assure you,' he said, extending his hand. 'After all, I do realise that you're on a holiday and you had—er ...' his eyebrow quirked provocatively, 'other plans for your leisure time than working.' He pulled her to her feet. 'Now let's get on with it before you change your mind. Go back to your room and change first, and I'll treat you to lunch.'

'I never did thank you for breakfast the other day,' she remembered as he gathered up her towel and her hat.

'Purely a business expenditure,' he returned, his eyes sparkling so that she could not be certain whether or not he was serious. 'I had already developed the photos I took on the beach and knew I wanted more.'

'Oh,' Megan felt a slight disappointment that his interest in her was only professional, and then she tried to shrug it aside. At least the trip wouldn't be a total waste. She would *definitely* have something to write her room-mates about now!

Marc followed her inside her bungalow, enquiring, 'Do you mind if I use your phone to call in?'

'No, help yourself.' She selected a pair of peach-coloured slacks from the closet, and a pale green tee-shirt, over which she would wear a voile blouse printed with tiny peach and green flowers. She went into the bathroom to change.

She heard Marc on the phone through the paper-thin walls. 'Gayle, I'm bringing home an ingénue in about an hour. I want you to set up for a standard two-hour session, and clear everybody out. Absolute privacy. Oh, and make reservations for two tonight at the Yardarm, will you? Thanks very much.'

Megan came out and he was sitting on the edge of the bed, taking in the furnishings of the small room with the same alert interest with which he observed everything. 'Very foresighted of you,' he commented, 'to rent a separate cabin. Much more privacy that way.'

She turned away quickly to search through a drawer for a scarf. She found it, a long green chiffon, and quickly looped it about her neck. 'I'm ready,' she announced.

Marc gave her a mocking look which turned her words into a double-entendre. 'Are you quite sure about that?'

She picked up her handbag, annoyance flashing in her eyes. 'Let's go,' she said.

Marc slipped his arm about her waist casually as they walked towards the hotel. 'We'll just have a quick bite to eat at the hotel, if you don't mind,' he said. 'I have a full schedule this afternoon.'

'Maybe another day would be better,' she suggested, a little too quickly, and at his enquiring look, she confessed, 'I'm not too sure about this. I mean, I don't know why you want to photograph me—there's nothing special about me, I'm very ordinary-looking . . .'

Marc laughed and drew her closer. 'Darling, how sweet! No,' he told her more seriously, 'every woman has something special about her, and you perhaps more than many. You just leave it up to me to find those special qualities and capture them on film. All you have to do is be your sweet, unassuming, adorable self, and all will come out right.'

'I wish you'd stop saying I'm sweet!' she complained. 'You don't know anything about me. Everybody says I'm "sweet".'

'Can everybody be wrong?' he queried. 'There are worse things to be, you know. Like promiscuous,' he suggested with a devilish gleam.

Megan jerked away from him with an angry exclamation, and he chuckled lightly. They walked the rest of the way to the hotel without conversation.

Marc ordered without consulting her, a salad for each of them, tea for himself, coffee for her. This annoyed her more than usual because she had skipped breakfast and was really very hungry. 'I had a salad for dinner last night,' she told him. 'You might at least have asked me what I wanted!'

'It was a very sexist thing to do,' he admitted. 'But we always eat light before a session. I can't have you falling asleep under those hot lights.'

'More likely I'll pass out from malnutrition,' she muttered. Already she could tell Marc was everything she disliked about a man—chauvinistic, domineering, insincere, and a user of women ... But his one kiss had given her a glimpse of sensuality she had never imagined before, his simple presence seemed to charge the air with electric virility, and she was as much a victim to his well-practised charm as any other woman who had ever walked the earth. Perhaps that was what disturbed her most about him—he had the effortless ability to make her feel like nothing more, and nothing less, than a woman. She knew she should resent him for that.

'No,' he countered her order when she asked the waiter for another cup of coffee, 'we should be going up. Gayle should have everything set up by now.'

'Gayle?' queried Megan, looking longingly after the waiter as he retreated with the coffee pot. 'Your secretary?'

'Perfectly indispensable fellow,' he answered, coming around to help her with her chair. 'I couldn't operate without him.'

She stared at him. 'Gayle?' she repeated incredulously. 'Your secretary is a man?'

'But of course,' he answered, draping his arm lightly about her shoulders as they started for the elevator. 'All the best secretaries are men, didn't you know that?'

'I most certainly did not!' she objected heatedly.

'Certainly. The Secretary of State, the Secretary of Defence . . .' Megan almost giggled, but then he went on, perfectly seriously, 'Female secretaries have a tendency to be skittish, if you know what I mean. I need someone who can keep a level head on his shoulders, manage my hectic schedule, take care of all the hundreds of little details that can make or break a session—all without flying into hysterics at the drop of a hat. With a man, I can be sure of reliable, efficient and consistent service, while a woman can be depended upon to be none of those things.' She stared at him, seething, and he continued blandly, 'You can expect a woman to be absentminded and irritable about once a month, like clockwork, not to mention the unpredictable bouts of tears and temper over the latest crisis in their love lives, or their unfortunate tendency to get pregnant at the most inconvenient times . . .'

Megan could take it no longer. 'If you have such a low opinion of women,' she said sharply, 'it's a wonder you can bear to work with them as closely as you do!'

Mark looked incredulous. 'Low opinion of women? My dear, I adore them! They're truly the most delightful creatures ever fashioned, and the things I love most about them are the very reasons I would never employ one in a responsible position.'

'For your information,' she retorted as he ushered her into the elevator, 'women are employed in professions of responsibility all over the world—women doctors, lawyers, senators, even a Supreme Court justice! Your Queen,' she declared triumphantly, 'is a woman!'

'Wonderful the way that worked out, isn't it?' he replied. 'Queens should always be women. And,' he added with an endearing smile, 'vice versa.'

'You're infuriating!' she told him. 'A single man like you could put the cause of women's rights back half a century! I don't think I want to work with you after all.'

'Too late,' he announced as the elevator opened and he guided her into the corridor with a light pressure on her back. 'Let's finish this delightful discussion at a later date, shall we? I'm very serious about my work, and I can't be distracted with frivolities.'

Before Megan could retort, he had swung open the door to his room and ushered her inside.

The suite was enormous, decorated in sea colours of blue and green with touches of ornate gold in the carving of the mantel and the trim on the lamps and tasselled throw cushions. The colour scheme directed attention to a huge picture window with a breathtaking view of the beach below and the restless sea. The forward wall had been cleared of furniture and set up as a studio, with a glaring white backdrop in front of which rested a long, high pedestal covered with a white fur, and surrounded by spotlights and cameras. Through an open door Megan got a glimpse of a huge mahogany fourposter bed.

'All right, love,' said Marc, going forward to peer through each of the cameras in turn, occasionally making a slight adjustment, 'take off your clothes.'

She stared at him. The only word her numb lips would form was a blank, 'What?'

He did not glance up. 'Surely you don't expect me to photograph you dressed like that? Oh, it's very charming, I'm sure, and perfectly appropriate for lunch, but not at all what I had in mind.'

'But,' she stammered, 'but you said—that is, I said ... what I mean is,' she managed with a breath, 'is that I thought I'd be modelling clothes.'

'No, no,' he replied impatiently, stretching overhead to straighten a light. 'I told you, I have professionals for that. What I expect to capture is the real you.'

'Couldn't,' she ventured, 'you capture the real me—dressed?' And she was thinking desperately, You're a modern girl, don't be such a prude, but at the same time she knew she did not want to take her clothes off for this attractive, virile man, to have him standing over her with a camera in the bright lights, arranging her limbs this way and that ... No, she just couldn't do it.

He glanced at her as though for the first time

hearing her. A glint of amusement sparkled in his eyes. 'Now surely,' he said, 'a girl who's ready to go out and snare the first likely candidate she sees to take as her lover should have no qualms about posing in the nude for me.' And then, briskly, he turned back to the light. His tone was as professional and impersonal as that of a doctor. 'Leave your underthings on, or slip into one of those swimsuits you'll find in the bedroom. There's a large white sheet on the bed—wrap it around you. Hurry now, love, I haven't got all day.'

Megan retreated from the room, cautiously relieved.

She left on her undergarments and found a swimsuit that fitted, then returned to the room with the bulky sheet wrapped tightly about her. Mark helped her on to the pedestal and arranged her silently in the position he wanted, stepped back to turn on the lights, and then came to her again, tilting her face slightly. The look in his eyes was very absorbed as he studied her face, and she sensed immediately the withdrawal into himself. For him, she no longer existed except as an object to be photographed, and the lengths to which he would go to achieve the effect he wanted on film should not be taken personally. His absorbing, searching examination of her face did seem more than that—as though he were peering into the depths of her soul—and though she knew it was only his method, she could not stop a faint tingle of a blush from creeping into her cheeks.

'Beautiful,' he whispered, still probing her eyes. 'I love a girl who can blush—there are so few of them left . . .' His fingers stroked her face lightly.

'Yes, beautiful . . . no make-up, how perfect, but perhaps just a touch of gloss. . .' Without removing his glance or the strong, gentle fingers that stroked her cheek, he dipped his finger into a pot of peach-coloured gloss that rested on a pedestal nearby and touched her lips. 'Yes, kissable lips . . . soft, moist, eager for love . . .' His finger caressed her parted lips with feather-strokes, sensuous and provocative, a foreplay to love. But his voice was a monologue of hypnotic quality, his eyes those of an actor very much and very convincingly into his role. 'Have those lips ever been kissed?' he murmured softly. 'Are they perhaps waiting for their first kiss, eager, expectant, welcoming . . . Don't move now, love, don't even breathe . . .' He backed slowly away, reaching for a camera; the shutter began to click rapidly. 'Beautiful, beautiful!'

The time that followed transported Megan into a world without time or space, the mesmerising quality of his soothing monologue her guide, and in that endless afternoon she began to understand what it might feel like to be in love. She did not experience the discomfort of the hot lights, for even when Marc came forward to blot her skin lightly with dusting powder or to fluff her hair with tender, caressing fingers he did not break the spell. Only later would she realise the aching muscles caused by sitting for long times in unaccustomed positions, for now she was totally captivated by the spell that was Marc Campion.

The sheet was arranged high under her arms, but though he had fluffed and draped it many different times during the session, never had its arrangement given a hint of anything that was not entirely modest. Now he came forward, still deep into his role, and stood very close to her, his hands gently caressing her shoulders.

'And now, darling,' he said softly, 'we're on the verge of total surrender . . . will you, or will you not? Can you keep the promise your eyes have made, or will you hold your secrets for ever to yourself?' Even his words could cause her pulse to race; she could believe for a moment that they were not in a studio at all beneath glaring white lamps, and that he was sincere. His eyes could transport her to believe in his sincerity.

His hands moved slowly to the top of the sheet. His eyes held her. 'Now, love, I'm going to do something that may frighten you a little, and it's only natural to be frightened, because you've never been this far before . . .' Slowly, he began to tuck the top of the sheet into her swimsuit, his fingers warm against her skin.

Megan's heart began to pound. She could not break the eye contact. 'Will I hurt you?' he whispered, very close to her now, his presence and his warmth completely engulfing her, filling all her senses. His fingers folded down the sheet another fraction. 'Will my passion for what you've so long withheld completely overrule my sensibility? Or will I be gentle with you, as you deserve . . .?'

Her heart was choking off her breath as he folded down the sheet another inch, her lips parted and she felt colour building in her face, though whether from embarrassment or something else, it was impossible to tell. His fingers brushed against

her bare breasts as he made the last adjustment to
the sheet, folding it to just above her nipples, and
though the light touch caused a shiver to break out
on her arms, she wondered if he was even aware of
it. 'No, darling,' he said, very softly, 'you have
nothing to fear, because you know I'll take no
more from you than you're willing to give . . .' He
reached for a brush from the make-up stand
without ever allowing his eyes to leave her face,
and gently drew a line of blusher between her
breasts with the sensuous, whisper-light stroke of
the bristle. 'No, enchanting child,' he murmured as
he began to back away, 'we're on the threshold of
a great adventure, you and I, and you need have
no fear, for the man who teaches you will teach
you well . . .'

The shutter began to click, and Megan forced
herself to block off the sound of his crooning voice
which already had had such a devastating effect on
her. She must not allow herself to be so easily
enchanted, she must not become another one of
his victims . . .

It was over.

Marc cast the camera aside and came over to
her, arms extended to help her down. 'I do
apologise, I've kept you much longer than I
intended—you must be exhausted!'

Megan hastily rearranged the sheet and grasped
his shoulders as he swung her down, admitting,
'No, it was fascinating, really.'

'Well, you run along now and change,' he said,
giving her a light slap on the bottom—exactly as
one might to a child. 'And then go home and soak in
a hot tub. If you don't you'll be aching all over in a

few hours, and we have reservations for dinner at eight.'

She turned back to him. 'We do?'

'Of course.' He was busy with the cameras again. 'We have a fascinating philosophical discussion to finish, remember?'

Megan smiled to herself and went into the bedroom.

She was a little slow changing, because her thoughts were so much with the man in the other room, the power, the fascination of him. How could anyone act so well, and switch it off so quickly and finally when the role was no longer necessary? Every motion he made, every word he uttered was an act of ultimate sensuality. But that was only the role he played. She thought she knew a little about the real man—arrogant, opinionated, self-assured and narrow-minded. The two sides of his personality clashed drastically, but still she was a little uneasy, wondering if there were not a point where the two men converged into one ... wondering if she would always be able to tell them apart.

When she came out, he was already working with another model. She was tall and slim, possessed of a beautiful mane of long red hair which Marc was now tousling with his fingers as he murmured, 'There it is—the bedroom look. Provocative, maddening, wild ... completely wild ...' The shutter began to click, and Megan watched in fascination.

The girl was wearing a sleek strapless one-piece over which was a sheer ankle-length wrapper. Mark pushed the wrapper from her shoulders so that it draped on her elbows, all the time talking to her—just as he had talked to Megan, using some of the same phrases. He moved one of her slim, haute-couture legs on to the pedestal, bent at the knee, and folded her hands across it. He arranged her cheek to rest on her hands, fluffing out her hair, saying, 'Tell me what you want, darling, let me see it in your eyes . . . that's it! I know what you want, and it's this . . .' He bent over her, encircling her with his free arm, and kissed her deeply and for a long time on the mouth.

Megan felt colour flash to her cheeks and she turned quickly to go. The word 'operator' had just been given an entirely new meaning. When she thought how close she had come to succumbing to that phoney charm her eyes snapped and her colour deepened.

So intent was she upon making her angry escape through the door that she almost did not notice the other woman lounging near it, observing coolly both the proceedings in the studio and Megan's reaction. Megan took her for another model—she had the tall, elegant, half-starved look, her frosted hair was clipped above the ears and moulded sleekly to her head, her make-up was heavily though expertly applied, and her cranberry silk kimono looked very expensive. She was smiling at Megan in a humourless, superior way.

'You're new, aren't you?' she enquired.

Megan answered only, 'Yes,' and brushed by her.

'He does have a weakness for the young ones,' the other woman commented. 'I suppose you're completely captivated.'

Megan drew herself up and regarded her coolly. 'I certainly am not! His technique is—well rehearsed and very effective, but I never for a moment imagined it was anything else.'

The woman's smile deepened at the corners, but she said nothing else as Megan opened the door. Then, as though answering a question Megan had not asked, she said, 'Oh, yes, he's a *very* good lover.'

Megan stopped and looked back at her.

The woman simply regarded her with that same cool, knowing smile, and added, 'That *is* what you were wondering, isn't it?'

Megan left the room quickly, trying to deny that it was true.

CHAPTER FOUR

SEVERAL times that afternoon Megan thought of calling Marc's hotel and cancelling their dinner. But she knew that was being childish. It was his method, just as she had told the cool woman in his room, and she had no reason to be offended just because he used the same technique with other women besides herself. This was the twentieth century, after all, things like this went on all the time, and she really had to get with it. Marc Campion was attractive, charming and exciting, there was no reason why she should not enjoy his company and take what he offered at face value. The old-fashioned standards by which she was accustomed to judging men were no longer appropriate ... things like sincerity, reliability and permanence just really weren't important. She was free to spend her time—a day, a week, or a month—with whomever she chose, without being hampered by such things as suitability or compatibility or what type of husband he would eventually make. That was one of the nice things about being a modern woman.

Accordingly, she went to great lengths to prepare herself for this date. The sun had already brought out the golden highlights in her hair, and she washed it and brushed it until it gleamed. She pinned it back with the coral combs just as she had the night before, and applied just a touch more make-up to emphasise her high cheekbones and wide eyes. She wore a clinging jersey dress of deep plum, its full skirt swinging just above her calves and clinging to the outline of her slender hips and thighs when she walked. It was strapless, gathered at the waist and at the top into a modified blouson effect, and trimmed with a tiny row of ivory crocheted lace. Around her throat she fastened a simple velvet ribbon of the same plum colour, ornamented with a small, modest gold brooch. She wore small gold studs in her pierced ears, and a single gold bracelet on her arm. She dabbed just a trace of perfume behind her ears, on her wrists, behind her knees, between her breasts. Then she looped her lace shawl over her elbows and looked in the full-length closet mirror. The total effect was stunning. She could hardly believe it was her.

Marc rapped sharply on her door at precisely seven-thirty. She did not keep him waiting.

A white dinner jacket complements some men more than others, and Marc was one of the fortunate ones. Its crisp whiteness was the perfect contrast for his dark colouring. It brought the crystal blue of his eyes to sparkling life and emphasised romantic shadows on other parts of his face. Megan had not fully appreciated before how long and thick his eyelashes were, nor how the lower lashes were so dark they seemed to be an artistic smudge highlighting the beauty of his eyes. The correctly folded dark tie sported a small, winking ruby pin which drew attention to the romantic red streak running through his hair from parting to temple. Megan knew she would be the envy of every woman they passed tonight, and she felt a little thrill as she saw his eyes take in her appearance warmly and then register approval. Approval from a man like Marc Campion meant a great deal—perhaps far too much.

'My dear,' he exclaimed vibrantly, taking her hands, 'you look exquisite!' He leaned forward and lightly kissed her cheek. Even so casual a caress as that caused her breath to quicken.

He stood for a moment, smiling down at her warmly, then slipped his arm about her waist. 'We'd best go,' he said. 'Although the temptation to keep you all to myself tonight is very great.'

Megan tried to hide a tingling thrill of pleasure. She was glad she had not cancelled the date, and wondered now what she had ever been piqued about. All she sought was a little fun, and tonight she intended to have it.

Marc escorted her to the car, his fingers warm and caressing about her small waist, and too soon he reminded her of the turbulent emotions she had experienced upon leaving his room that afternoon. 'What did you think of the session?' he asked.

She slid into the squat, low-roofed vehicle and the sensuous memories of the afternoon came tumbling back, topped with their insulting climax. She replied, 'I was impressed. I never dreamed anyone could be so phoney, and do it so well.'

His glance was glinting with amusement as he sat behind the wheel beside her and started the engine. 'Phoney? My dear, I'm hurt! I'm never anything of the kind!'

'Maybe you do it so well that you fool even yourself,' she replied with just a touch of petulance.

'Hardly,' he insisted. 'I'm quite sincere about everything I say at the time I say it ...' Then, frowning a little, 'Not that I always remember what I say when I'm shooting. Did I manage to offend you this afternoon, pet? Say something out of line?'

Megan stared at him in incredulous exasperation. This man was really incredible! How could she stay angry with him? She shook her head helplessly at last and answered, 'No. Nothing out of line.'

'Oh, I'm so glad to hear it,' he answered with patent relief, 'because I only want to ask you whether you'll sit for me again and then we'll put all thought of work behind us and enjoy this perfectly lovely evening together. Will you?'

She hesitated, but only for a moment. Then, before she committed herself completely, she said, 'Just tell me one thing honestly.'

His eyes were like sapphires in the lights of a passing car as he looked at her. 'Anything,' he promised.

'This afternoon—when you first asked me—did you really intend for me to pose in the nude?'

Marc chuckled as he turned back to the road. 'Not for a moment, lovey. Not,' he assured her with a penetrating glance that swept her briefly from neckline to ankle, 'that I'm not convinced your nude body is a perfect delight—I've seen most of it, anyway—but, as I told you, I don't work that way.'

She caught on that one phrase. 'What do you mean,' she demanded in alarm, 'you've seen most of it?'

'Those wicked little bikinis you wear. Surely the most provocative garment ever yet designed by man, and, for your information, capable of arousing far more lust in the male breast than simple nudity can ever hope to do.' He chuckled again softly to himself. 'I did have you going for a moment there, didn't I? Perhaps you're not quite so liberated as you supposed.'

Megan squirmed uncomfortably. The passing lights of bright store fronts in the shopping district reflected a rosy colour on her cheeks. 'You'll never know,' she retorted defiantly. '*You* were the one who backed down, remember?'

His eyebrow quirked as he cast her a sidelong glance. 'That statement,' he told her, 'could put some very unscrupulous ideas in my head regarding the next session ... however I won't tease you. I would never dream of asking any of my models to pose nude, much less a charming little ingénue like yourself.'

She was not quite certain what he meant by 'ingénue', but she bristled anyway. 'Why "much less" me? I'm no different from anyone else!'

'Because,' he assured her, reaching for her hand, 'the corruption of your innocence would be for ever on my conscience.' She tried to snatch her hand away, but he held it firm. 'I had,' he added softly, caressing her again with his eyes up and down, 'much rather discover the wonder of your unclothed body in more natural circumstances.'

Her heart tightened in her throat, and she wondered if he were once again only putting her on. It frightened her a little because she did not think so.

And then he said, still holding her hand, 'Have I frightened you off, or will you agree to sit for me again?'

Her hesitancy lasted a little longer this time. If she said no, what were her chances of ever seeing him again? If she said yes, would she eventually graduate to the position of that other model she had seen in his arms? The possibility both excited and appalled her. Did she really want his attention under those circumstances, shallow and insincere, no better than the last time he had kissed her and she had discovered it had all been a joke? She heard her voice responding, 'Yes, I will.' Perhaps it was the memory of that last kiss.

Marc squeezed her fingers. 'Perfect! Now let's forget all about work and spend the evening discovering pleasanter things about one another. Do you like seafood?'

Megan glanced at him, laughing a little at the abrupt change of subject. 'Well, yes . . .'

'Excellent.' He released her hand to swing the car into a parking space in front of a long, low building which seemed to be constructed entirely of glistening white coral. 'You're about to taste seafood unlike any you've sampled before . . .'

They passed beneath the yellow lamplight that spilled over the entrance and stood for only a moment beneath an enormous ship's wheel before the maître d' noticed them and hurried forward, greeting Marc by name and ushering them to their table. Megan had always dreamed of going to a place like this with a man like Marc, receiving solicitous attention from superior waiters whose weekly salaries probably doubled hers, but she could not quite believe it was really happening. The interior was lit only by the red lanterns which reflected off white tablecloths, and the atmosphere was intimate and subdued. They were shown a corner table, slightly secluded from the other couples, who conversed softly or simply held one another's hands and exuded a soft privacy of their own. Marc pronounced the table to be satisfactory, and the maître d' took Megan's shawl.

'Would you care for an aperitif?' Marc asked in response to the waiter's question, and Megan, who was not quite certain what an aperitif was, graciously declined.

They looked at one another for a moment, Megan's eyes sparkling with excitement, Marc's serenely content. The atmosphere around them was intimate and romantic, and just as Megan was slipping blissfully into the aura of fantasies-come-true, a voice from over his shoulder caused Marc to turn his head.

Megan looked up to see one of those incredibly beautiful women approaching. She could have been one of Marc's models, but her figure was full and soft, and Megan did not think so. She was simply one of those gorgeous, glamorous and sophisticated women with whom Megan had begun to associate Marc—and who, she suspected, were drawn to him like metal shavings to a magnet.

The woman's voice was husky and well trained into a pretence of boredom, but there was an unmistakable undertone of delight there as she exclaimed softly, 'Marc darling! I thought it must be you but I could hardly believe my eyes!'

Marc stood quickly, and Megan did not miss the appreciative light in his eyes as they fell on the other woman, nor the warmth in his voice as he replied, 'Priscilla! What a delightful surprise!' and Megan's heart sank as he clasped both of the woman's hands and kissed her lingeringly on the cheek. 'What brings you here?'

'Oh,' she replied negligently, though her eyes still shone with a subtle light as they met Marc's, 'I'm cruising with the DuValls. We only anchored yesterday for a week in the islands ... I don't suppose there's any chance you might join us?' Her eyes brightened with the possibility, and Marc still held her hands. 'What a frolic that would be! We're doing the entire Caribbean, you know, and it's such a fun group ... Rodney and Alicia, Stephanie and Dolores, and Adam Brand—you know Adam, don't you, dear? But we're simply not complete without you—do say you'll come!'

'Alas, dearest,' he replied with a sigh that Megan was not entirely certain was exaggerated, 'I'm only a working chap and haven't time for a holiday.' And then, as though suddenly remembering Megan's presence, he dropped one of Priscilla's hands and turned back to the table. 'Forgive me, I can't think where my manners have gone. Prissy, love, allow me to introduce Megan Brown. Megan, Priscilla Ambrose, a very dear friend.'

The effort to reply with a polite smile was enormous as Megan took in the woman's golden tan, the strapless white evening gown which floated about her curvaceous body like gossamer, the sleek dark hair and the perfectly applied make-up. What could Marc see in Megan after looking at a woman such as Priscilla Ambrose? Only a small town girl, she thought in despair, dowdy and unsophisticated, totally unworthy of his notice.

Reluctantly, Priscilla said goodbye and went to join her party in the other room, but Megan could not help noticing the look she shared with Marc before she left, which seemed intimate, and the way Marc's eyes followed her across the room. Megan could never compete with a woman like that, or with the dozens of beautiful, glamorous women to whom Marc was accustomed. She felt vaguely depressed.

But when he was seated again, turning to her with a gentle smile, it was all too easy to look into those crystal eyes and imagine no such person as Priscilla Ambrose had ever existed. He looked at her and she wanted to believe she was the only woman in the room; when he smiled at her she could believe it.

'I wish you could see what this light does to your eyes,' he said softly. 'They're enormous. And totally captivating.'

Happiness leapt in her, and a tingle began in her fingertips. After all, they were alone together, even if it was for this moment and no more, and she wanted to savour it, relaxing in the warm spell of the charm he exuded. But her pleasure was modified by caution. She lowered her eyes briefly and felt compelled to make the light retort, 'And you're wishing you had your camera.'

'No,' he replied gently, reaching for her hand. 'Not tonight.'

His fingers closed about her in a warm and gentle grip, and Megan felt herself sinking inexorably into utter contentment. And just then the menus arrived. 'I strongly recommend the lobster,' said Marc, glancing over it while she studied hers. 'However . . .' His eyes met hers over the menu with a teasing glint, 'I won't act the sexist tonight. You may order whatever you like.'

Her lips curved upwards despite her attempt to fight a smile, and she folded the menu. 'The lobster sounds fine,' she told him.

Marc ordered for them quickly, as though anxious to be rid of the intruding presence of the waiter, and then turned back to her. 'You see,' he said mildly, 'that proves my point. It's every woman's secret wish to be dominated by a man.'

She gaped at him. 'That—that's ridiculous!'

'Nature itself is an example,' he assured her. 'The female of the species is eternally dependent on the male for food and defence while she's nursing her young.'

'The lioness,' she exclaimed triumphantly, 'provides food for her own cubs while the lion is off who knows where!'

His eyes danced maddeningly. 'Ah, but don't forget that without the lion there would be no cubs.'

'Don't change the subject,' she defended irrationally.

Marc was having difficulty restraining his laughter. 'All right, I won't. Throughout nature you'll find that the female is designed as the weaker sex, orientated to home and hearth, dependent on and submissive to her male counterpart.'

'I object to that!'

'Object all you like, lovey, but it doesn't change the facts. It's a woman's destiny to ultimately surrender herself to a man, and that moment of surrender, when it does come, is a moment of purest ecstasy ...' His sparkling eyes winked at her with restrained mirth. 'Now may I change the subject, or shall I go into a detailed lecture of the coupling habits of Burmese tigers?'

'Oh,' she exclaimed, torn between annoyance and the almost irrepressible desire to laugh herself, 'you're impossible!'

'Now,' he suggested, 'may we move on to less volatile topics? Tell me about your home town, Megan.'

She laughed lightly. 'You could hardly have chosen a less volatile subject than that! It's very, very dull.'

'But charming,' he insisted.

She lifted her shoulders lightly. 'Your typical middle America town. Population about five thousand, every one of which five thousand people knows the business of every one of the other four thousand nine hundred and ninty nine ... Nothing very interesting at all.'

'It is to me,' Marc insisted. 'And what's the name of this charming little burg?'

'Apple Corners, Maryland.'

He exclaimed, 'Delightful!' and she giggled.

'And do you live at home?' he prompted. 'Any brothers or sisters?'

'Just my parents and myself,' she answered. 'I work in the doctor's office there. I like my work,' she defended, realising it must sound very boring to him. 'I could have gotten a job in Baltimore—

it's only about twenty miles away and most of the people in Apple Corners commute—but I preferred to work in a less formal office. When I get back, though,' she told him, 'I've decided to move to Baltimore, get an apartment there, and *commute* to Apple Corners! That will be a change! I'm really tired of small town life,' she confided. 'I don't want to leave my job, but I just can't take living at home any more.'

'What a pity,' he said, 'that so often we can't appreciate the value of what we have when we're in the midst of it. But of course you're right,' he added, as though anxious to avoid a dispute. 'It's time you asserted your independence.'

The waiter brought their wine, and Marc paused to taste it. He pronounced it satisfactory, and the waiter poured two glasses.

'I guess you travel all over the world,' said Megan when they were once again alone, and there was a touch of envy to her tone.

'Paris, Rome, Cairo, Vienna . . . And if I sound a little jaded, dearest, it's because I am. I should like nothing more than to be free to enjoy the small town life you've just described to me.'

She repeated, puzzled, 'Free? There's hardly anything *free* about living in a small town—or private! It's positively boring!'

'Freedom means different things to different people,' Marc answered, 'for, you see, we all struggle with our separate bonds. To you, of course,' he added without a flicker of expression to betray whether or not he was baiting her, 'freedom means a cheap bed-sitter and a series of one-night stands . . . I wonder how long it will be, my dear girl, before you realise the folly of your choice.'

'That's not fair!' she objected heatedly. 'You make it sound like ... like ... it's not that way at all! All I'm saying is that I'm tired of being kept in a glass cage, and I should be allowed to do whatever I please with my life, and that marriage is not the only choice open to me.'

'What about what's currently termed, I believe, "a meaningful relationship"?' he asked. 'Is there room for that in your plans?'

Megan took his question seriously. 'I think,' she decided, 'that would be as bad as being married. I don't need a relationship to keep my life going.'

'This George fellow,' he suggested, 'must have done something terrible to turn you against men so completely at your age.'

She ignored the reference to her age and felt compelled, for some reason, to defend George. 'Oh, he's not so bad. Just very ordinary. He just made me see how very *dull* it would be to be married. And also,' she added, 'how easily I can get along without him.'

Any rebuttal Marc might have made was interrupted at that moment by the arrival of the lobster. Megan tackled it with enthusiasm, and he watched her in amusement. 'How refreshing to see a girl with a healthy appetite!' he exclaimed.

'Well,' she defended, 'I've hardly eaten anything at all today, and it *is* delicious.'

'You're utterly charming,' he told her, and turned to his own meal.

Megan reflected that she had much rather be referred to as 'fascinating' or 'dangerous' or even 'mysterious', but she decided not to let that mar her evening.

The food was rich, and the wine heady. Her eyes took on a deep sparkle which, had she known it, was more than a little fascinating. Marc responded to her mood and treated her just as he might any other woman—one of his elegant models, for example, or the fast, alluring woman of the international set. When they left the restaurant, he did not take her immediately to the car, but guided her instead around the back of the building, where there was a fragrant, enclosed garden.

Megan drew in her breath at the moonlit beauty. The air was redolent with the scents of cedar and allspice, and artfully constructed beds of hibiscus and red and white poinsettia gleamed in the silvery light. Far in the distance was the whispering of the surf, and when Marc drew her to him with an arm about her shoulders, they seemed to be effectively sealed away from the outside world and into this haven of fragrant beauty. 'Such a setting becomes you, angel,' he said softly. 'Eve in the Garden of Eden, innocent and uncorrupted. Would that you could remain so for ever!'

Her heart had begun to beat just a little faster at the tender tone of his words, the warm strength of arm about her. She managed to reply, a little uncertainly, 'Eve didn't.'

He smiled, 'And has given women a bad reputation ever since!'

They strolled along the shell paths of their leisure, and she wondered if he would kiss her. Even the thought made her go weak with anticipation, and she knew she hoped he would. As they made the full circle and returned again to the gate, Marc bent and snapped off a glowing croton, then placed it gently in her hair.

He looked at her tenderly for a long time, and she felt her colour rise in joyful eagerness as his eyes rested longingly on her lips. And then he said softly, 'Ah, little darling! There's so little left in this world that's pure and untouched . . . why do you insist upon throwing away one of life's dearest treasures so thoughtlessly?'

She flushed, not from anticipation now, but from embarrassment. Her disappointment was so acute it hurt. She could feel his eyes upon her for a moment longer, and then he said abruptly, 'We'd best be back. Morning light comes all too soon.'

Still, against all likelihood, Megan wondered whether he might turn the car into the hotel parking lot. Of course he did not, but continued the few hundred yards down the street to the group of bungalows. He helped her out of the car and walked with her in unnatural silence to the door. She could not recall ever having felt quite so awkward before, not since her first date at the age of sixteen. She did not know what to say, or what to do. At last, under the small eave which served to deflect the frequent island rains, she turned to look at him.

He rested one arm casually against the door frame, the look he bent on her was reflective and tender. And then he asked softly, 'May I kiss you goodnight?'

She caught her breath. This was the moment she had been waiting for, and she must not spoil it with words, nonetheless they slipped past her, urged on perhaps by the memory of last night, and a more recent, more unpleasant memory. 'Is it customary to ask?' she retorted.

Marc's dimple was very deep with the small, lopsided smile. 'One always asks permission of impressionable young virgins,' he assured her, 'unless one is preparing to act the cad, as I did last night. It's only etiquette.'

She turned casually away from him. 'I take it by that that the woman I saw you with this afternoon was not an impressionable virgin.'

There was a puzzled silence, then a soft laugh. 'You must mean Adrienne. Were you still around then?'

She flared. He had forgotten about her so soon!

'No,' he told her, a trace of laughter still in his voice, 'the only description which fits Adrienne is "young". And she expects to be treated exactly the way I treated her—it's the only way she'll respond.'

'Oh, I'm certain,' Megan returned sarcastically, 'that you're an expert on discovering how to get women to respond *exactly* as you want them to.'

'It's my profession,' he assured her. One finger reached out to lightly trace a pattern on her arm. She felt an unwilling shiver begin as his warm touch teased her flesh. 'Now, will you give me your answer, or shall I take your maidenly reluctance as silent consent?'

Megan turned to him boldly. 'You may kiss me,' she said.

He took a step forward and drew her lightly into his arms. With one finger he tilted her chin upward, and her heart began to pound as she felt her own arms encircling his broad chest, the fine material of his jacket beneath her fingers. His lips touched hers.

Her response was immediate and instinctive, and it surprised even herself. Last night had been only a hint of the delights in store, and even though it had ended tragically, the sweet memory was not dimmed. She was ready for him, and eager for more.

Perhaps Marc was caught off guard, for almost immediately she felt his breath quicken at her response, the light embrace tightened gradually until she was pressed fully against the hard length of him, his mouth opened to engulf hers and she was drawn deeper into the sensual experience. She lifted her arms to encircle his neck, loving the feel of his silky hair beneath her fingers, and her shawl dropped into a graceful heap at their feet. His fingers caressed her bare shoulders and her back, and she could feel the steady beating of his heart against her breast. When he lifted his face at last it was only to drop more kisses, quick and gentle, on her eyelids, the corner of her jaw, her collarbone ... she could feel his breath warm against her chest and then his lips in the soft valley between her breasts. She moaned softly, clinging to him, afraid if she did not her legs would be unable to support her. Then he pressed his lips passionately to her neck, his hands hard and firm upon her head beneath her hair, and a dizzy wash of emotion began in the centre of her abdomen and swept upwards like none she had ever known.

He murmured, 'You're dangerous, woman-child ... much, much more than you know.'

Then he lifted his face and drew her head gently to his chest. Megan felt his fingers softly untangling her curls, and then his lips on her hair. She simply lay against him, holding him, her breath unsteady, her entire body quivering.

Then he pushed her a little away, smiled down at her, and took her key from her hand. He unlocked the door.

She looked at him, her eyes wide and uncertain, a little afraid of what lay ahead, but still dizzied by the warmth of his embrace and the passion he had so recently stirred to life. And then, surprisingly, he pressed the key in her hand.

'I'll call you tomorrow,' he said.

She stared after him as he started to turn away. Somehow, she found her voice, although it was very weak and small and not like her own voice at all. 'Won't—won't you come in?' she managed.

Marc turned back to her. The expression in his eyes was tender, and a little sad. Then he bent and kissed her cheek softly. His lips lingered against her skin a moment longer, then he straightened up. 'Goodnight, Megan,' he said.

CHAPTER FIVE

THE sound of the surf outside her bungalow was like a soothing lullaby, but Megan could not sleep. The events of the day had left her too disturbed. She had come here with nothing more in mind than a little light summer romance, for the express purpose of expanding her horizons and obtaining some of the sophistication of which she felt she was so badly in need. She had met the man of her dreams and everything should have been perfect ... but somehow it wasn't. Somehow things were not working out at all the way she had planned.

She sighed and turned restlessly on her side, bunching up the cool pillow under her cheek. Was this the way a modern girl approached the business of romance? Did she lie awake nights dreaming of crystal blue eyes and an engaging smile? Did she yearn for his touch and feel as though her heart would break whenever they parted? No, the modern woman did not become involved, she looked only for the good times and took them wherever she could find them ... which was exactly what Megan had intended to do. Only it was turning out to be much more difficult than she had expected.

She was becoming too involved with Marc Campion, and she was very much afraid it was too late to turn back now. Until this point Megan's experience with men had consisted of high-school sweethearts, a few uneventful casual dates with men her own age introduced by mutual friends . . . and George. What did she know of vital, exciting men like Marc Campion? She was very much afraid she had got in over her head, and the worst of it was, she was beginning to care for him—far too much. For the one thing she had not considered when she had embarked upon the adventure of a lighthearted romance was that the day would come when she would have to say a lighthearted goodbye.

It simply was not working out at all the way she had expected.

She moaned softly and pulled the pillow over her head, and when at last a restless sleep came it was troubled by dreams of a tall, dark-haired man with laughing blue eyes.

She was awakened at dawn by a pounding on her door. While she was drowsily orientating herself to time and place and hoping the annoying noise would soon cease, she heard Marc's voice call cheerfully, 'Rise and shine, poppet! Let's not waste the morning light!'

She scurried out of bed and ran to the door in her nightgown, not bothering to pull on a wrapper. 'Marc!' she exclaimed, and drew him quickly inside. 'What are you doing here? You're going to wake everyone in the complex—what in the world will the neighbours think?'

His eyes glinted amusement. 'Not half,' he assured her, 'what they would think if they could see you entertaining gentlemen callers in your bedroom wearing nothing but that skimpy little nightie.'

Megan blushed as she remembered what she had worn to bed the night before—a spaghetti-strapped baby-doll of clinging acetate which barely covered the lace edging on her panties. 'Never mind that now, love,' he told her as she went quickly for a robe, 'the damage has already been done. I've invaded the sanctity of your lingerie and there's no recalling it now.'

She turned to him, and she could not prevent a burst of laughter. 'You're a nut!' she told him.

'Now, where have I heard that before?' he mused.

She placed her hands on her hips, her head cocked to one side, and demanded, 'What *are* you doing here?'

'I've come,' he announced, 'to take you swimming.' He caught her arm and spun her towards the bathroom. 'Hurry and change now, love, let's not keep the tide waiting.'

'Does it?' she retorted, pausing to snatch a swimsuit from her drawer. 'Wait, I mean.'

'Only at my command,' he assured her.

She slipped into a satin-finished orange bikini which was drawn to nothingness at both sides of the hips and between the bra cups by delicate gold buckles. She remembered Marc's comment about bikinis from the night before and was a little more selfconscious about it than she had ever been previously, but she had not brought any other style of swimsuit. *He* could hardly lecture on modesty, however, she observed as she pulled on her beach wrapper and came back into the room. Beneath his open white muslin shirt he was wearing one of the smallest pairs of swimming briefs she had ever seen on a man. Only someone with his trim, athletic build could have got away with it. The scanty white garment only emphasised his vital masculinity, the firm muscles of his abdomen with his diminishing triangle of crisp dark hair, the sinewy strength of his thighs, the trimness of his waist and hips without an ounce of excess flesh.

She thought her assessment of the appeal of his various parts had been covert, but when she looked up to tell him she was ready to go, his eyes were dancing wickedly, just as though he had read her thoughts and was vastly amused by them. He slipped his arm about her shoulders in a way that seemed more patronising than affectionate, and said lightly, 'Come along, then, poppet, let's go.'

'I wish you wouldn't call me that,' she complained as they stepped out into the warm morning light.

'Call you what?' he queried.

'Poppet. What does it mean, anyway?'

'I'm not quite sure,' he replied. 'I believe it generally refers to something sweet and cuddly and altogether quite adorable. And it suits you.'

Megan frowned. 'Well, I don't like to be thought of as cuddly and adorable.'

'And how would you rather be thought of?' he insisted politely.

'Oh,' she mused, scrunching up her toes in the night-cooled sand. 'I don't know. Mysterious, maybe, or exciting, or unpredictable . . .'

'Fascinating, alluring, unforgettable?' he suggested.

'Exactly.'

'But, darling, you are all those things!'

'No, I'm not,' she replied unhappily. 'I'm not cool, or dignified, or aloof . . .'

'Well, I must agree with you there,' Marc replied, and she shot a challenging look at him, for every woman expects to be contradicted when she says unflattering things about herself.

She caught the warning twinkle in his eye just before he swept her off her feet and into his arms, running with her into the tide until the cool surf splashed on her legs and soaked the bottom of her bikini. She squealed and squirmed in mock protest which turned to genuine protest as he prepared to drop her into the not-quite-warm water. A moment later his arms released her and the cold shock of a wave swept over her. She came up sputtering and groping for him, and he drew her into his arms, his body slippery and, despite the fact that he was as wet as she, still warm. 'No,' he told her laughing, 'you're not at all dignified or aloof!' And then he pulled her down as another large breaker formed and rolled towards them.

Beneath the water, drifting for that briefest moment with the tide, she felt his lips press hers. In that salty, silent underworld they were for a fraction of a second one body, borne along with the timeless effort of the sea towards a destiny unknown. And then the wave broke, and he lifted her high into the air, laughing, and let her drop again into the crest of a wave.

They frolicked in the breakers for a time, then swam out a little, where the gentle undulations of the sea allowed them to turn on their backs and float, aimlessly and dreamily, with the drifting currents. Marc held her hand, drawing it on to his chest, and she felt the protective strength of his fingers about hers and the wet mat of hair beneath them and knew she had never been happier in her life.

The huge rocks along the shoreline, sculpted by centuries of wind and water into fantastic monoliths, pillars and grottoes, glowed red and gold in the morning sun as they at last turned and swam in. The beach was still deserted, and it looked like a fairyland designed exclusively for their pleasure. As Megan struggled out of the sucking surf, breathless from the exertion, Marc caught her about the waist and pulled her down on to the wet sand. She collapsed there, breathing hard and laughing, as the water tugged at her curls and tickled as it seeped beneath her. He lay beside her, one arm about her waist, the other propped beneath his cheek as he watched her, his eyes bright and avid.

'What a sheer joy you are!' he exclaimed softly. 'Your love of life is reflected in everything that you do—in every part of that delectable little body—but most especially in your eyes. What a tragedy it would be for you ever to lose that quality.'

'Lose it?' she laughed, turning her face towards his. 'I don't even know what you're talking about.'

'It's this,' he replied, very earnestly. He sat up, so that now his posture was more like a lecturer than potential lover, although the tightening of his hand about her waist left room for doubt. 'You will take the advice of almost a dozen years I have on you, poppet—and yes, I will call you that, because that's what you'll always be to me—and don't open yourself up so easily for hurt. Enough of it finds us of its own accord, without our going out to seek it. There's someone ahead for you—maybe a long way down the road, maybe just around the corner. And this person will teach you love the only way it can be taught, with tenderness and caring, and you'll become a part of him and he of you—not just for a moment, but for always. To settle for less would be foolish, Megan. To seek less is to cheapen yourself and destroy the very thing about you which makes you so special—your unquestioning acceptance of life. Because you *will* be hurt. That lovely light will die from your eyes and they'll become hard and bitter. Lines of disappointment will grow on your face where there should be lines of laughter. And your smile will no longer enchant with its openness and freshness—it will become cool, and too wise of things you never should have learned. Ah, Megan, can't you see what tragedy that would be?'

She was touched by the words, and confused, and strangely hurt—for the tone he used was concerned but almost fatherly. She did not want to hear that tone in his voice when he spoke to her. She did not want to think of him as a father—or a brother. So she quipped, shifting her eyes away from his, 'I hardly see how any of it concerns you at all. Since you've already very graciously disqualified yourself for the position, you have no right to lecture me on what kind of lover I should or should not take.'

Marc's eyes twinkled. 'But that's *exactly* what

gives me the right,' he told her. 'I have nothing to lose, so I'm perfectly unbiased.' He seized her hands and drew her to her feet. 'Now I have to get to work,' he said briskly. 'Go back and change, and when you've breakfasted come on up to my room. I've set aside some time for you this morning.'

Megan showered and changed thoughtfully, and something deep within her was aware that the fascination Marc Campion held for her had gone beyond that. He was more than just a startlingly attractive man, an electric personality, a romantic charmer. He was, she gradually came to realise, everything she had always dreamed of, and more. She had found the place where his two personalities converged—it was gentle and tender and caring, and it drew her with a power like none she had ever known. All she knew was that she would be content to spend every minute of her day with him . . . and that he thought of her as no more than a child. A very foolish child, at that.

Her mood was not very high as she finished breakfast in the hotel dining room, despite the fact that her anticipation of being in Marc's presence again made her fingers tingle and her cheeks feel hot. How much more foolish he would think her if he knew that the mysterious lover she sought was, in fact, only him.

As she stepped out of the elevator, the door to Marc's suite was open and the scene that greeted her was quite different from the one she had encountered the day before. Models crowded the doorway in various states of attire and spilled out into the hall. Some were wearing swimsuits, others robes or chiffon cover-ups, one was wearing what, from Megan's point of view, looked like little more than a G-strap and she made no attempt to cover herself. Just outside the door the woman who had addressed Megan so coldly the day before was scolding one blonde girl in a short kimono severely.

'Look at you!' she exclaimed. There was venomous contempt in her voice and her eyes. 'Do you really think Marc will let you within three feet of a camera looking like that? What were you up to last night,' she sneered, 'or need I ask?'

The girl defended, 'I didn't realise this was a prison camp! I'm old enough to come and go as I please!'

'And you look every year of it!' the woman shot back. 'You look, as a matter of fact, like you've been dragged through a bar and had a swing at every wino in the place!'

'You can't talk to me like that——'

'I can and I will! Unless,' the woman suggested dangerously, 'you'd rather hear it from Marc, and I can assure you he won't be nearly as gentle with you as I'm being!' The girl seemed to shrink a little as this threat sank home, but the other woman did not lighten her tirade. 'You're being paid good wages for this assignment, and a man like Marc Campion expects his money's worth! Not,' she spat, 'some low-priced callgirl with circles under her eyes that would make an owl jealous and skin that looks like it came from a pastry factory!'

With a cry of rage, the blonde drew back her arm. The other woman caught it fiercely in mid-swing and whirled her around. 'Get back to your room,' she snapped, 'and stay there. And you can be sure Marc will hear about this—we'll just see how quick you are to swing at me then!'

The girl broke away and fled past Megan, sobbing.

Megan was appalled. She suddenly realised that to reach Marc she would have to brave that lioness and push through the huddle of girls who had only now resumed a cautious, disturbed murmur of conversation. She was just considering turning back to the elevator when the woman spotted her. 'You!' she called, and began to break away from the crowd. Megan could not ignore the fact that she was addressing her, and she turned to face her, squaring her shoulders and painting a pleasant smile on her face. 'You were here yesterday, weren't you?' she said, as she reached her.

Megan replied, 'Yes, I was.'

The other woman scrutinised her carefully, and suddenly Megan felt awkward, dowdy, and underdressed in comparison with the other's sleek elegance. Her make-up was expertly applied, from the deep crease of charcoal on her lids to the cranberry lip gloss and blusher, she was wearing tight satin slacks and an almost transparent flesh-coloured shirt tied at the midriff. She was not wearing a bra.

She told Megan abruptly, 'We're not ready for you yet,' and turned to go. Then she hesitated, and turned back. 'Maybe you'd better wait inside,' she said, but there was still no warmth in her voice.

Megan followed her as she broke a path through the girls at the doorway. They crossed the room and circled the studio area, where Marc was working very closely with the model on the pedestal. He did not notice her.

'My name is Olivette Carlisle,' said the woman as they entered the bedroom and she closed the door. 'I have some tea warming; would you like a cup?'

'Thank you,' replied Megan, 'that would be nice.' She sat in one of the gold brocade chairs that had been drawn up around a serving table in the centre of the room while Olivette Carlisle poured the tea. 'My name is Megan Brown, by the way,' she added.

'Yes,' smiled the woman enigmatically. 'Marc has mentioned you.' There was something very intimate about the way she spoke Marc's name— something that made a chill run down Megan's spine. 'You're not a model, obviously,' she added as she lounged back in the other chair.

'No,' admitted Megan, and sipped her tea. It was very hot.

'You must be another one of Marc's pick-ups, then,' Olivette commented smoothly.

Megan jerked her head up. 'I certainly am not! I——'

The woman laughed. It was a cool, brittle sound. 'No, darling, I don't mean "pick-up" in the usual derogatory sense. It's simply that Marc has a penchant for wandering about and bringing home waifs—any little thing that happens to strike his fancy. We call them pick-ups, as opposed to professional models. Sometimes he photographs them,' she added meaningfully, 'sometimes he doesn't.'

The tea suddenly tasted bitter, and Megan set

her cup down. She folded her slightly damp hands in her lap and made an effort to be polite. 'You've worked with Marc for a long time?'

'Oh, ages,' the other woman replied, waving a hand lazily. 'Marc and I have been together for ever.'

There was an implied threat in those words that Megan could not miss. 'Marc and I have been together for ever,' it said, 'and we always will be, so don't try to come between us . . .' Megan hoped she was misunderstanding. But the cold light in Olivette's eyes was unmistakable.

She lifted her cup to her lips, never once freeing Megan from that unnerving gaze, and said casually, 'I suppose you're already in love with him.'

Megan tightened her hands together and tried to force down a flush. But she was no good at hiding her feelings. Olivette drawled with a small smile, 'I thought so. Very unwise of you, my dear, if you'll allow me to advise. Very unwise indeed.'

Just then the door opened following a short rap, and a tall, thin, balding man poked his head in. 'We're ready for Miss Brown,' he announced.

'My dear,' said Olivette lazily, 'have you met the incomparable Gayle Winters? Marc's secretary.'

Megan turned to the man who looked more like a very correct butler than a secretary, and said, 'How do you do?'

He acknowledged her with a short nod.

'How does he want her dressed?' enquired Olivette.

'He doesn't,' replied Gayle, and closed the door behind him.

'That means you're to go as you are,' explained Olivette unnecessarily, and they both rose. 'We'll talk again,' she promised Megan.

It was a promise Megan hoped she would forget.

Marc bent forward and kissed her cheek gently as he helped her to the platform. 'Wonderful to see you again, lovey,' he smiled. 'I've been counting the minutes.'

'I could tell,' responded Megan drily. Already she could tell this session would be drastically different from the one the day before. It would not be so easy to fall victim to his act with all these people milling around.

'Jealousy doesn't become you, sweet,' he told her, his eyes still smiling into hers. He dipped and brushed her lips lightly with his. 'Now, how are you?' he asked softly, drawing the intimacy about them. 'Relaxed? Anything bothering you?'

'I'm fine,' she answered, although it was not strictly true. The interview with the enigmatic Olivette still disturbed her, but she felt its effects slowly dissolving beneath his charm.

'Terrific!' He backed away from her to make an adjustment on the lights. 'We're doing face shots today, but later on we'll go out beneath the sun or the stars or the moon or whatever you like and do some action shooting. Would you like that?'

His voice had already taken on the soft, hypnotic timbre, and Megan was not certain whether it was wise to disturb him while he was building the mood. But she asked curiously, 'Marc—what are you going to do with all these pictures? Will you sell them or something? Will they go in a magazine?'

'They will go,' he replied, returning to her, 'into my private portfolio.' She must have looked disappointed, for he assured her, 'I always keep my sweetest treasures to myself, like a hungry old miser ...' He bent close to her, withdrawing further and further into himself. 'I love that hint of a sunburn you have across your face,' he told her. 'It makes your eyes so clear I can see right through them and into your soul. Perhaps just a touch of oil across the bridge of the nose ...' He made a slight, quick motion with his hand, and Gayle came forward to sweep something that looked like a small paintbrush across her face. 'Excellent, excellent!' He began to back away, shutter clicking. 'Now you're drifting free on an unmoored yacht, the sea is your home, the sun is your dreams ... perhaps we should try the fan ...' From somewhere a silent, high-powered fan switched on, blowing her curls about her forehead and her cheekbones. 'Lean back for me, darling, on your elbows, turn your face up, but whatever you do don't close those gorgeous eyes ... what are you seeing, sweetheart? Who are you dreaming of?' And then, abruptly, 'No, no, that's not it. Turn it off.'

The fan wound down, and Megan sat up, afraid that his impatience was directed at her. But when he stepped on the platform he merely drew her to him with one arm about her shoulders in a reassuring squeeze, and his eyes were tender. 'It's not working, is it, love?' he said softly, smiling. 'The chemistry isn't there.' Then, more loudly, turning away but not releasing his protective embrace, 'All right, clear everyone out. Be quick about it!' Then he turned back to her, squeezing her shoulders again briefly. 'Only a moment, love.'

Gayle moved very quickly, and in less than a minute the room was emptied of models, stray garments, and unnecessary equipment. The door closed on them in silence.

'Now, sweetheart, let's begin again.' Marc kissed her nose lightly and stepped down.

For a time the session progressed normally, and Megan let herself be swept away by the mesmerising tone of his voice, not hearing the words, only the soothing quality. She knew that if she listened to the words she would be lost, for she had fallen too much under his spell already. And gradually she could not help herself.

He commanded softly, 'Listen to me, darling, listen to me and believe what I say. Those eyes, those captivating, scintillating eyes ... what secrets do they hide? Dare I believe what I see in those eyes? Is it—can it be—an invitation? Or something more, something far more dangerous .·. if I lose myself in those eyes will I be lost for ever? Or will I see only the reflection of myself wanting you, loving you, needing you for my very existence ...'

Her heart began to tighten in her throat. She wanted to cry, 'No, no, don't say that!' Because he did not know how badly she wanted to hear those words from him, but to hear them *for real*, not as part of an act designed to get a response from her ...

'Those lips ... aching to be kissed, making me

ache with desire for you ... That face, so innocent, ready to be taught, yearning to be taught, and it's I who teach you, love, and only I ...'

Marc never remembered what he said while he was shooting: Megan tried to tell herself that. He meant none of it. If only he could know how he was hurting her by saying those things she longed so desperately to hear, and meaning none of them! If only he knew, he would think her a fool. She felt tears begin to sting her eyes. She was afraid he would notice if she tried to blink them back.

'That face! I adore every millimetre of that face ... I want to hold it in my hands and kiss it until it cries out for wanting me ... just as I want you, my only love, my dear sweet innocent, how I want you ...'

It was no use. The tears spilled over and streamed down her cheeks, into her parted lips, splashing on to her chest as she bowed her head. They came faster and faster, blurring her vision, and she was helpless to stop them. Marc slowly put the camera aside and came over to her.

She thought he would scold her, or make fun of her, and she was wretched with embarrassment and hurt. Now he would know, now he would only laugh to himself when he thought of her, now she would never see him again ...

Self-defence turned hurt into anger, and she lashed out at him as he reached for her, a gentle gesture which reminded her too much of the way one might comfort a child. 'Leave me alone!' she cried, pushing his arms away. Her eyes flashed behind the film of tears. 'You think you're so clever, don't you? You can use your silver tongue and your phoney charm to get anything you want from a woman—tenderness, passion, or . . .' She swallowed hard and determinedly on a new lump in her throat. 'Or tears,' she finished defiantly, anger at herself and at him building steadily. 'Well, it won't work on me any more! I don't like being used and I'm not going to be another one of your toy dolls, so—just leave me alone!'

She jumped down from the pedestal and almost fell. Marc caught her quickly, and as she looked up at him, her face still flushed with anger and streaked with tears, she thought she saw a momentary confusion in his eyes—again there was a glimpse of that place where the actor became a real man, and everything within her softened towards it.

Then it was gone. His smile was gentle but his tone condescending as he patted her arm and said, 'You're tired. I've been working you much too hard.'

Megan bit back a retort, already regretting her flare of temper which had necessitated his making excuses for her. But oh, how she hated the indulgence in his voice!

'Perhaps you'd like to go back to your bungalow and nap for a while?' he suggested.

She drew away from him. 'Maybe I'd better,' she agreed stiffly.

His arm encircled her shoulders as he walked her to the door, completely oblivious to the turmoil inside her. 'Although,' he added, 'I'm not at all sure I want to let you out of my sight, even for so brief a time.'

For a wild moment hope flared, and her eyes swept eagerly to his. The hurt and the anger evaporated as she experienced a flash of pure joy, hoping it might be true ... 'Why?' she whispered breathlessly.

'Because,' he responded lightly, 'I feel it my bounden duty to the other hapless members of my sex to protect them from your ruthless designs. As long as you're with me, the remainder of the male population on this island can rest safely.'

The hurt that ripped through her was like the cut of a searing sword from the pit of her stomach to her heart. The wild hope of ecstasy plummeted out of sight. Pain bubbled up within her numbly and she repeated to herself, 'Only a game with him, only a game ... I mean nothing to him and I never will ... It's only a game.'

She stepped slowly away from his embrace, and gathered up her purse from one of the entrance tables where she had left it. Then she turned back to him with a tight, rather strained smile. 'You don't have to worry about the other men,' she told him. She lied to him as he had lied to her. 'They're safe enough.'

'I'll give you a call later, love,' he called after her.

'Fine,' she replied, and closed the door behind her.

She spent most of the afternoon trying to get him out of her system. She cried a little, but mostly she lay on her bed and stared at the ceiling. She had come to the island to declare her independence and to prove to everyone she was capable of making her own decisions, and she had rushed headlong into the worst possible blunder. She had fallen in love with a man who not only did not love her, but who would never think of her as anything more than a charming child.

Then, about five o'clock, she made another decision. She had been trying to convince herself all this time she was a modern girl, when in fact she had behaved like nothing more than the old-fashioned heroine of a classic romance. Falling in love was foolish and outdated. Modern women did not lose their hearts to dashing, romantic men with red streaks in their hair—modern women took fun and companionship where they could find it, and awoke the next morning with neither regret nor guilt. And that was exactly what she was going to do.

There was one dress in her wardrobe she had never worn. She had bought it out of wild, defiant impulse, and had vaguely thought she might find the courage to wear it on this trip, where no one knew her and could think what they liked. She knew it was extremely sexy, and was not even certain it was tasteful, but tonight she would throw caution to the wind. She put it on.

It was a bright fuchsia triacetate knit with a shimmery finish, and it moulded itself to her body despite its full cut. It was fashioned somewhat like a Roman toga, pinned over the left shoulder from a sweeping diagonal bodice with a flashy zircon. It was gathered at the waist and fell to the calf, but was slit up the left side from hem to hip. Its clinging quality would tell a man immediately that she was not wearing a bra, and make him wonder whether she was wearing anything else at all beneath it. Her legs were good, and so were her breasts, firm and rounded and not too large, but when she looked in the mirror a small expression of trepidation crossed her face. She dismissed it quickly.

While she was dressing, the telephone rang. It must have rung fifteen times, but Megan gritted her teeth and ignored it. It was a while, though, before she could continue dressing.

She pinned her hair up off her neck so that the curls tumbled with wild abandon over her forehead, then she applied a daring, dark shade of lipstick and blusher, very much like that Olivette Carlisle had worn that afternoon. As a final touch, she found a pair of long, fan-shaped dangle earrings set with clear zircons. She looked, she thought, at least ten years older, and very sophisticated.

Just as she was preparing to leave, the phone rang again. She couldn't stand it after the sixth ring, and jerked it off the receiver. For a moment she didn't know what she would do if it were Marc's voice . . . and who else could it be?

'Miss Brown? This is Gayle Winters, Mr Campion's secretary.'

His secretary!

'Mr Campion would like to ascertain whether you're free for dinner this evening, and suggests he call for you in an hour.'

His secretary! He had had his *secretary* call to make a date with her, probably because *he* was too busy. But not too busy to keep a paternal eye on her!

'Please convey my thanks to Mr Campion for

the invitation,' replied Megan with pleasant formality, 'but unfortunately I have other plans for the evening. Perhaps another time.'

She hung up the phone with a sort of bitter satisfaction.

The sun was beginning to set over the water as she drew her shawl about her and walked quickly to the hotel. It reminded her of the enchanting pink and gold sunrise she had shared with Marc this morning ... how different the world had seemed this morning!

Megan had never been to a lounge by herself before, and she was not quite certain how to behave. The interior of the Sea Winds was dark and already moderately crowded, and would it be more proper to try to find a table, or to sit at the bar? Proper, she thought in self-derision, was *not* what she had come here to be! She sat at the bar.

The bartender asked for her order, and for a moment her mind went completely blank. What were those exotic, sexy-sounding drinks continental women always ordered? She couldn't think of one. Finally, aware of his patience, she ordered a glass of white wine, and was glad to have it to sip on as she looked covertly about the place.

It was of course decorated with a seafaring theme, with ships' wheels and brass bells and lanterns swinging from the ceiling giving off a very mute light. Over the windows was pasted a sort of ripply blue material which was meant to give the effect of underwater portholes. That, combined with the smoky air, effectively diminished the lighting to a bare hint. And then Megan felt someone sit beside her.

'Hi,' he said. 'Are you waiting for someone?'

She looked up, a small shaft of panic shooting through her. She had not expected it to happen this fast! He was blond, and nice enough looking, dressed in a leisure suit with a casually unbuttoned print shirt. The all-American swinger, she thought.

She cleared her throat a little and replied, 'No. No, I'm alone.' She looked back to her drink, her mind working in a sort of muted panic. This was the way a modern girl met men, then. This was what she had intended to do in the first place, and she would have been here days ago if it hadn't been for Marc ... but she refused to let thoughts of Marc intrude. If she thought of him she would never have the courage to go through with it ... and she would go through with it—wouldn't she? After all, she was an adult and this was what she wanted, wasn't it?

He asked, 'Do you want to spend some time together?'

Megan shot a startled glance at him. It *did* move fast! Well, she told herself with an inner breath of determination, this is your chance ... 'All—all right,' she managed, and tried to smile.

He smiled back. 'My name's John.'

Sure, she thought. John *Smith*, no doubt. Oh, how could she ever have been so foolish? she thought with an unexpected little shaft of despair. This was not how she had expected it to be, a quick pick-up in a bar with a man she doubted very much she would even like if she knew him ... and did she really think she could make love with a man she did not even *know*? Yes, she told herself determinedly, reaching once again for a firm grip on her courage. This was how it was done. 'I'm Megan,' she answered him as pleasantly as she could, but found she could not look at him for more than a moment. She turned back to her drink.

'Vacation?'

She nodded. This *was* what she wanted, she told herself fiercely. No involvements, no commitments, free and light and totally modern. She had nothing to be ashamed of, no one was looking over her shoulder, and things like this happened every day. It was the way of the world. She tried to relax.

'This is my last night,' he was saying. 'I'm flying back to Omaha in the morning, but . . .' now his smile was insinuating, 'I have a feeling this is going to be the best night of the whole trip!'

Well, she thought, trying to bolster her courage, that makes it convenient. One-night stand, no long goodbyes . . . exactly what she had wanted. She managed another weak smile.

'What are you drinking?'

She sipped again, delicately. The wine had lost its flavour. 'Wine,' she answered. 'White.'

He grinned. 'Classy!' He signalled for the bartender and ordered another glass for her, a Tom Collins for himself.

He turned back to her. 'So, Megan, do you like to dance?'

She nodded. 'Sure.' She thought, I wish I were anywhere else . . .

'Fine,' he replied, and his voice lowered a fraction, became more intimate. 'I know a place, not far from here, where the band is good . . .' She felt his hand on her knee. 'And after that . . .' His fingers began to crawl up her leg, and tried not to squirm away. 'Who knows?'

She had never imagined it would be like this. In her plans and daydreams it had been so easy, so carefree . . . But in reality she had never been more embarrassed or uncomfortable in her life. How did all those modern women do it?

But again she took a firm hold on her courage. She was beginning to sound to herself like the dull, inexperienced, dreadfully boring girl she had left behind in Apple Corners. And she wasn't. She was enlightened and sophisticated and anxious to embrace every experience with open arms. 'Yes,' she answered him with a brave smile. 'Who knows?'

His hand was on her thigh now. It felt hot and damp, and she found herself wondering irrationally whether he was wrinkling her dress. 'What do you say,' he urged, 'we get out of here——'

And just then she heard a cold, familiar voice behind her. 'I beg your pardon, sir, but I think there's been a mistake.'

Megan whirled to meet Marc's dark, expression-less face just as his fingers closed tightly about her upper arm. 'The lady is with me,' he said.

'Hey, wait a minute . . .' But John's heated protests dissolved into bluster as he took in Marc's size and the deadly anger in his tone. He turned back to his drink, muttering.

'Come along, dear,' Marc said smoothly, but his grip on her arm was far from gentle and he pulled her off the stool with a jerk that almost caused her to lose her balance.

Her cheeks flooded with humiliation and rage as

he led her across the floor. He was walking so fast
he was almost dragging her. She made a weak
attempt to break away, but found she could not do
so without making a scene, and for a moment she
was too furious to even speak.

'How—how *dare* you!' she choked at last as they
were in the corridor. She made a concentrated
effort to pull away. 'Let me go! What right have
you . . . you have no right!'

Marc walked to the lift and stabbed the button,
his fingers digging into the flesh of her arm. His
jaw was set in a hard line, and he did not look at
her.

'Just who do you think you are!' she cried,
righteous anger building now. 'Nobody asked you
to interfere! It's none of your business—none at
all! How dare you!'

The lift opened and he shoved her inside. They
were alone as the doors closed and she began to
splutter again, 'Let me go! What do you think
you're doing? You have no right——'

He looked at her, and that look silenced her.
She had never seen eyes like that before; they were
like chips of ice. He said tensely, 'Shut up.'

Megan gasped.

The doors opened on to Marc's floor and he
dragged her down the corridor. He opened the
door to his suite and propelled her inside with a
force that almost sent her sprawling. She caught
herself against the sofa as the door slammed
behind him with a blast that caused the little
crystal ornaments on the lamps to tinkle. Despite
her fear of the dark fury she saw being unleashed
in his face, she turned to attack again. 'Well, I

think you have a lot of explaining to do!' she cried, rubbing her bruised arm. 'Just what do you mean, bursting in there and dragging me away from my date—you don't own me——'

'No,' he shot back, 'it's *you* who have the explaining to do, pet! What were *you* doing there, dressed like a strumpet and smelling like a cat-house——'

She gasped audibly.

'Making eyes at the first four-handed wolf who comes along!'

'It—it's none of your business how I dress, or——'

'Except to note,' he returned viciously, 'that women who go into bars looking like you do right now generally end their evenings with more money than they began them with!'

A hot rage of insult and mortification swept through her. 'How—dare you——'

'Yes,' he shouted, 'I dare! Someone had damn well better! It's none of my concern whether you intend to lose your virginity to a gigolo or a leper, but you might at least go about the matter with a little taste! Why not parade around a prison camp naked or play chicken on a freeway—both of which occupations would be a lot safer than picking up a strange man at a bar, I can assure you! You might have at least chosen one that wasn't married!'

'M-married?' she stammered, momentarily disconcerted.

'Don't tell me you didn't notice his wedding ring?' he sneered. 'The fool didn't even have the good taste to take it off!'

Megan lifted her chin defiantly, although she was quaking inside at the cold dark fury that was turning his face into that of a man she had never known before. 'It doesn't matter,' she told him. 'And even if it did, it's none of your business——'

'For God's sake, take off that disgusting dress! You look like a child masquerading in her mother's best clothes—although I don't know a mother worth the calling who'd be caught dead in something like that! Take it off!'

She gasped and shrank back. 'I will not!'

'You were going to do it for *him*, weren't you?' Marc closed the distance between them in three angry strides. 'Why not for me?'

He grasped the flimsy material at the shoulder clasp and she cried out and tried to jerk away. She sobbed out loud in humiliation and fear as the fabric fell away with a gentle ripping sound, baring her breasts. 'Stop it!' she cried, struggling to cover herself as she wrestled against the firm grip he had on her shoulders. 'Leave me alone! You can't——'

He shoved her roughly towards the bedroom. 'Put some clothes on,' he growled.

She fled, trembling, to the relative safety of the bedroom. Anger and fear were blurring her eyes, and she was hot all over with embarrassment. Her fingers shook as she scrambled through a pile of model's clothes, finding nothing more suitable than a white terry beach cover-up. She tried to calm herself as she slipped it on, and stepped out of her dress. The dress was completely ruined, but it didn't matter. She never wanted to see it again. She only wanted to get out of here and forget this entire wretched night . . .

She whirled as she heard Marc's angry footsteps behind her, fumbling to draw the robe together over her lace panties. But he did not give her a chance. He hardly seemed to notice her nakedness as he strode over to her and grasped her with one hand behind her neck, while with the other he began to scrub her face violently with a damp cloth.

'It appears,' he spat tightly, 'that I *will* have to keep you under lock and key, after all, because you've certainly proved tonight that you're incapable of taking care of yourself!'

Megan cried out in protest and tried to squirm away, but his furious scrubbing only increased. His hand on the back of her neck felt like a vice. Soap got in her eyes and tears of pain and humiliation welled up. He was treating her like a child—like no more than a naughty child! 'Stop it!' she sobbed. 'You're hurting me!'

'No!' he returned, but he flung the washcloth angrily into a corner. 'This is gentle compared to what might have happened to you tonight if you'd gone through with your little scheme! You think about that, Megan!'

'Let me go!' she wailed miserably, trying to wrench away. The sobs were uncontrollable now, and her humiliation was complete. She had never been so wretched in her entire life.

He released the pressure on her neck, but drew her instead against his chest with an iron-hard embrace. She felt a long, unsteady breath escape him through her own gulping sobs, and after a time he began to lightly stroke her back. 'Oh, Megan,' he muttered. 'Foolish, impulsive little Megan . . . What will happen to you?'

He lifted her wet face, and the look he bent on her was no longer angry. His eyes were filled with raw emotion—confusion, tenderness, compassion. 'Why did you do it, Megan?' he insisted.

She could not answer him. She dropped her eyes.

Then she felt his lips on hers, gently, and her breath caught. She felt his own tensing as the kiss became deeper, his arms tightened about her until her breasts were crushed against the buttons of his shirt, but she did not feel the pain. His arms were like steel bands around her ribs, choking off her breath, the hungry demand of his mouth was dizzying, flooding her veins with fire and her senses with electricity. His hands roamed through her hair and his mouth slid against her cheek as he murmured, 'How unwise you are, my dearest little Megan . . . Don't you know you can't give your body to a man without also giving your heart?'

The room was pulsating in shadows of light and dark as his mouth sought hers insistently again. She lost all track of time or sense of place, she lost the ability to reason or to exercise her will. The bed was only a few steps behind, and she found herself lying upon it, Marc's face only inches above hers as he whispered, 'I can show you delights you've never dreamed of, my darling . . . I can teach you love as it was meant to be . . . and when I'm done you'll be spoiled for other men, because you'll always belong only to me . . .'

He brought his mouth to hers again, urgently, and she felt his passion swell with hers as her lips parted beneath his insistent probing and she felt the moment of surrender sway near. He drew away from her, his eyes a very deep, fiery blue, and pushed the robe from her shoulders, bending to kiss each shoulder lightly, the nape of her neck until she shuddered, the hollow of her throat ... His hand travelled across the length of her almost-nude body to rest at length cupping her breast. And then she felt his tongue, warm and moist, delicately circling her nipple, a hot-and-cold flame undulated through her as his tongue traced a languorous path down her ribcage, across her abdomen, pressing a kiss on her navel and then into the sensitive hollow near her hipbone ... A moan escaped her and left her weak, pliable and helpless beneath the expert ministrations of his hands and lips.

He slipped one hand beneath the small of her back as his lips travelled upwards again, arching her into his strong, male length as his mouth covered hers again. Her arms twined about his neck and her fingers fanned against the silky softness of his hair, the hard muscles of his shoulders and the aching inside her was at once painful and pleasurable. But the overwhelming pleasure was simply being in his arms, feeling his nearness and the promise of his lips, loving him.

His lips slid to her cheek again, his breath warm and uneven against her face. Gradually the weight of his chest against her breasts lightened as he lifted himself to place long slow kisses all over her face, her eyelids, her nose, her chin, her forehead.

But beneath the overwhelming pleasure and the beautiful yearning he was creating within her there pounded a dim, unhappy realisation: he did not love her. He was only using her again, manipulat-

ing her just as he had from the beginning, only now
in a much more dangerous fashion. Megan turned
her face to stop the effect his caresses were having on
her, and when she looked back at him her eyes were
glittering. The pain and the humiliation of his
treatment of her was coming back with fresh clarity,
and she said, very distinctly, 'Is this how you make
your point, then?' Her voice was threatening to
break, but she would not give in to it. She stiffened
herself with remembered anger. 'So tell me, Marc,
what makes you so different from the man
downstairs—you both had only one thing on your
minds, right? You can lecture me all you want about
my morals—but right now I can't see that you're any
better than John!'

He sat up, and she felt tension coil in every muscle
of his body. Already she regretted her impulsive
rebuff, but she would not apologise. She was too hurt.

Slowly he drew the two parts of her robe
together over her. The expression in his violet blue
eyes was completely unreadable. 'I think,' he said
softly, 'that it would be safer for both of us if we
were on opposite sides of that locked door.'

For a moment Megan only lay there, stunned,
as he got up and crossed the room. Whatever
reaction she had intended to provoke, it had not
been this. She could not believe he was serious.
But she knew well enough when he opened the
door, and recovered herself sufficiently to cry,
'Marc!' just as it closed again.

She scrambled off the bed and ran to the door.
'Marc, wait! Don't——'

And then her disbelieving ears heard the bolt
click on the other side.

LOVE BEYOND REASON
There was a surprise in store for Amy!

Amy had thought nothing could be as perfect as the days she had shared with Vic Hoyt in New York City—before he took off for his Peace Corps assignment in Kenya.

Impulsively, Amy decided to follow. She was shocked to find Vic established in his new life... and interested in a new girl friend.

Amy faced a choice: be smart and go home... or stay and fight for the only man she would ever love.

MAN OF POWER
Sara took her role seriously

Although Sara had already planned her escap from the subservient positio in which her father's death had placed her, Morgan Haldane's timely appearan had definitely made it easie

All Morgan had asked in return was that she pose as h fiancée. He'd confessed to needing protection from his partner's wife, Louise, and t part of Sara's job proved ea

But unfortunately for Sa heart, Morgan hadn told her about Monique...

Your Romantic Adventure Starts Here.

THE LEO MAN
"He's every bit as sexy as his father!"

Her grandmother thought that description would appeal to Rowan, but Rowan was determined to avoid any friendship with the arrogant James Fraser.

Aboard his luxury yacht, that wasn't easy. When they were all shipwrecked on a tropical island, it proved impossible.

And besides, if it weren't for James, none of them would be alive. Rowan was confused. Was it merely gratitude that she now felt for this strong and rugged man?

THE WINDS OF WINTER
She'd had so much— now she had nothi

Anne didn't dwell on it, but the pain was still with her—th double-edged pain of grief and rejection.

It had greatly altered her; Anne barely resembled the girl who four years earlier ha left her husband, David. He probably wouldn't even recognize her—especially with another name.

Anne made up her mind. Sh just had to go to his house to discover if what she suspecte was true...

CHAPTER SIX

MEGAN tried the door. It rattled frantically, but did not budge.

He had locked her in !

The breathless passion of only a moment ago dissolved into coarse fury. She pounded on the door with both fists, shouting hoarsely, 'Marc! Open this door! You can't do this—Marc!' She kicked the door hard with her sandalled foot, repeatedly and with no effect. *'Marc!'* she screamed at the top of her voice.

At last she leaned against the door, breathless with the exercise, the wood cool against her cheek. No sound came from the other side.

Marc had locked the door and left her alone.

For a moment she considered screaming, pounding on the walls, even breaking a window. But that would only cause her more embarrassment, if, in fact, she were rescued at all, and she had had about all she could take for one night.

She gave the door one final, anticlimactical kick, and uttered a low, throaty sound of rage. Then she crossed the room and flung herself on to a chair.

Had Marc been only mocking her again? To treat her like a woman one moment, arousing all her womanly instincts to a feverish pitch, and then locking her in her room like a child the next! But no, she did not think even he could act so well.

What they had felt for one another in those breathless moments before had been real enough, and they were the feelings a man has for a woman, and she for him . . . then how could he *do* this to her?

She curled up miserably in the chair. Marc had said she couldn't be trusted out of his sight. Was this his way of driving home a cruel point, or of punishing his wayward child? He had, she realised with a pang of hunger which seemed totally inappropriate, sent her to bed without her supper!

She fumed and stormed for some time longer. She periodically walked over to the door and called, listening for some sign of occupancy on the other side. There was never any. As the hours wore on her anger exhausted itself; she was only tired and hungry and not very comfortable in a strange room with nothing to wear and not knowing what was going to happen next. She wandered over to the window and looked out for a while, watching couples stroll along the moonlit sand beside the foamy surf, remembering when she and Marc had walked together, that first night . . .

She watched a crescent moon rise high in the sky and begin to dip. There was still no sign of life on the other side of the locked door. Where could he have gone?

At last she went over to the bed and lay down. She fell asleep listening for the sound of his return.

It was his voice that woke her, bright and cheerful and very close. 'Good morning, poppet! Did you rest well?'

She sat up, rubbing her eyes, for a moment not remembering where she was. Morning light flooded the room, and Marc was coming towards her, carrying a breakfast tray with a single rose in a bud-vase surrounded by covered silver dishes.

'You!' she accused, her temper and her indignation stored up so well from last night flooding back with the memory. 'How *dare* you come waltzing in here, after what you did—how could you *do* such a thing!'

'Now, now, love, don't start throwing things,' he warned mildly. 'I come bearing gifts.'

'I'm surprised you can even *face* me after what you did!' she fumed. She scrambled to her knees, drawing the rumpled bed cover with her, as he approached. 'You've got some nerve! I've never been so——'

'I've a weakness for object lessons,' Marc admitted with a quirk of the eyebrow that suggested repressed amusement for her antics. 'But you'll forgive soon enough when you see what I've brought you.'

'I'll never forgive you,' she cried. 'Never! And stop laughing at me, you—you——'

'Cad?' he suggested, amusement now fairly dancing in his eyes as he set the tray on the table. 'Beast? Monster?'

Megan gave a low scream of rage and snatched up the pillow, but he wrestled it from her, laughing, before she could throw it. 'Now, then, love,' he declared when he had disarmed her of pillows, bedcovers and other throwable objects, 'are you quite spent? Got it all out of your system, have you?'

She glowered at him, pressing back against the headboard as though she found his very presence distasteful. 'No. There aren't enough dirty words to call someone like you, locking me up like a child after—after——'

He waved his hand impatiently. 'Oh, do let's put all that behind us. You're spoiling a perfectly gorgeous morning with your tantrums.'

Tantrums! Was that all her righteous indignation had meant to him—a tantrum? But of course, she was as always only a temperamental child to him, to be petted and pampered or coaxed or teased, whatever the mood required. Marc took nothing that had happened between them seriously, nothing . . . Megan felt her temper dissolve into a cold hurt, and her voice was stiff as she told him, 'You can sit in judgment on me if you like. You can mock me and manipulate me and treat me like a two-year-old and think you're all-wise and oh, so superior . . .' She blinked back angry tears and looked at him steadily, refusing to give in to another emotional display. 'But you just remember this. At least I've been perfectly honest about everything. I never lied to you or myself or anyone else about what I was doing, but you—you're so busy dishing out the phoney charm I doubt if you know what honesty is!'

For a moment something flickered across his eyes; he looked almost disconcerted. She felt a brief pang of satisfaction as she thought she had hit a nerve, but almost immediately the expression was gone. In its place was his usual flippancy, and he ignored her speech as though it had never been made.

'We're going to begin this day in style, love,' he declared, and took a bottle from the tray. He opened it with a muted pop, and a froth of bubbles streamed over the edge. 'Champagne!' He spilled some into two glasses and handed one to her.

'Champagne for breakfast?' scoffed Megan, but some of her bad temper was fading. She had never dreamed she would be having champagne for breakfast, and in the bed of an exciting, attractive, continental man like Marc Campion ... She accepted the glass.

'To your loveliness,' he toasted her, and his eyes smiled over the rim of the glass.

She tasted it, wrinkling her nose at the bubbles, as he placed his glass on the table and took up the tray. 'And that's not all,' he announced, arranging the tray across her lap. He removed one of the silver dishes. 'Strawberries!' He picked up three with his fingers and dropped them into her champagne. 'Delightful taste,' he assured her. 'Truly extraordinary.'

She tried not to show her pleasure. Strawberries and champagne for breakfast!

'And ...' he swept the cover off the larger dish, 'eggs Benedict!'

The rich aroma made her mouth water. She could hardly convey her anger with him while wolfing down the meal he had brought, but her stomach reminded her sharply of the missed meal the night before, and she did not think she could resist the temptation of the golden yellow sauce flowing over eggs and thick slices of ham ...

Her indecision must have shown in her eyes, for Marc did not prompt her any more. Her own near-starvation would save him the trouble. He sat beside her on the bed as she picked up her fork, pretending reluctance, and he reached for his glass. He waited until that first delicious bite had slipped down her throat and she was eagerly cutting another before he spoke.

'Now, Megan,' he said mildly, 'you have every right in the world to be angry with me, but I simply don't want to hear about it today. I have a most spectacular outing planned and I won't have you spoiling it by being sullen.'

She swallowed quickly and gulped her champagne. Every bite only reminded her of how ravenous she was. 'What outing?' she demanded.

He laughed softly and covered the top of her glass with his hand. 'Darling, that's champagne, not water! Don't drink it so fast! You'll end up tipsy and we won't be able to go anywhere.'

She made a wry face at him and turned back to her eggs. 'Go where?' she repeated.

'On a tour of the island. I'll be done shooting here in a couple of days, so I thought I could afford to take a holiday. The girls could use one too.'

Megan stopped with her fork in mid-air. 'Finished?' she queried. She looked at him, and her heart began to sink. 'You mean—you'll be going home?'

'Not home, not right away,' he replied. 'To New York, first, for a few days. Then London ... but you don't want to hear about that.'

But she did. She wanted desperately to hear about that. It was the first time she had given it a thought ... Marc would not be here for ever, and neither would she. He would be leaving soon, and she would never see him again. She forced herself to bring the fork to her mouth. The taste had disappeared, and so had her appetite.

Marc picked up a strawberry and absently twirled it in a cup of powdered sugar. 'Of course,' he added, almost as though to give her hope, 'my schedule is not entirely definite.' He popped the strawberry into his mouth, watching her. 'I may stay in the islands a bit longer than I'd planned. There's still plenty worth shooting.'

She turned back to her meal quickly before he could see the pleasure flood her face. All right then, if that was how it had to be, she would make the most of whatever time they had left . . .

A female voice from the outer room froze her in mid-delight. 'Marc? Are you in?'

'Here, darling,' he called back lazily, and Olivette Carlisle appeared at the door.

Her eyes took in at once the two of them breakfasting in bed, the champagne bottle, Megan's state of undress. A cold hatred hardened in her face which perhaps only Megan could see— it was the type of look one woman immediately recognises in another when they both love the same man.

But the expression was gone quickly as she lounged against the doorway and drawled, 'Really, darling, you must learn to close the bedroom door when you're entertaining!'

Marc's eyes twinkled back at her, unconcerned. 'What is it, love?'

'I only wanted to know what your plans were for the day,' she replied. Her cold eyes scanned

Megan up and down, and Megan felt utterly undressed and completely unnerved.

'I'm working with Megan,' he replied. 'We won't be needing. you.'

'So I see,' Olivette answered drily, and turned on one elegant heel and left the room. A moment later the outer door closed behind her.

Marc turned to her and grinned. 'Shall I bother to clean up your reputation, or does it bother you?'

She put aside her fork and took another sip of champagne, gathering courage before she spoke. 'Marc,' she said as casually as she could, 'who is she?'

'Olivette? I was under the impression you two knew one another.'

'Yes, but ... I mean ...' She wanted to ask, What does she mean to you? Instead she finished, 'What does she do?'

'She's one of those unfortunate creatures, too old to model, at loose ends, bitter with herself and the world, who's found compensation in persecuting girls younger than herself. She runs a modelling agency, and I work with her quite often.'

'You've known her a long time?' she pressed.

'Quite long, yes. Try the strawberries, love, they're delicious.'

Megan glanced at him. He was, as usual, immaculately dressed in a light grey blazer and slacks with a blue silk shirt and handkerchief which exactly matched the colour of his eyes. He looked well rested and refreshed ... not like a man who had been put out of his room and had spent the night wandering the streets. A sudden unbecoming curiosity overcame her, and she had to ask, 'Where did you sleep last night?'

He laughed. 'Is that really relevant?' He dipped his fingers into her glass and drew out a strawberry. 'Open!'

After a moment she did, and the strawberry was crisp and wonderfully exotic. She held out her glass for more champagne.

'No,' Marc decided, and removed her glass. 'You've had enough. And I'm anxious to get started before we lose the best light.'

'Oh,' she enquired as he lifted the tray, 'are you going to be photographing me today?'

'A bit.'

'When will I get to see the pictures? Have you developed any?'

'I don't always let my models see the finished product,' he replied enigmatically.

'Why not?'

He winked. 'It makes them too vain. Now, come along, love, get dressed and let's get moving.'

'But I don't have anything to wear!' she remembered. She did not even have anything to wear to travel back to her bungalow, unless Marc could supply something from one of his models' wardrobes.

'All taken care of,' he assured her, and disappeared into the other room.

He returned with a dress, and she knew immediately it was not borrowed from another girl's closet. It was a thin white voile, a shirtwaister with a full skirt and long, puffy sleeves. The high collar was trimmed with a self-ruffle, and the bodice was yoked and outlined with the same ruffle. A cascade of lace trimmed the sleeves and the ruffle at the hem. It was beautiful, feminine, and endearingly old-fashioned.

Megan drew in her breath softly. 'Is it for me?'

'Could you look at it and imagine anyone else wearing it?' he returned, smiling. 'I expect to see you in it often.'

'Oh, Marc . . .' she stood up and pressed the dress to her, 'it's beautiful!' But then she looked at him, deciding he deserved to be teased, for once. 'Are you sure it's proper for me to accept this?'

'What could be more proper,' he grinned, 'for the girl who's just got out of my bed?'

She laughed and made a playful threat to hit him.

'I've a pair of sandals for you too," he called as he made his laughing escape, 'but I may be wrong about the size.'

'How did you know the size of the dress?' she queried.

He winked at her again. 'It's my profession.'

The dress fitted to perfection, as did the sandals. Marc knocked on the door just as Megan was brushing the last tangles from her curls. 'About ready?' he asked.

She looked at him in the mirror. 'In this dress, I should be wearing a long blonde wig . . . you know, the fairy princess type.'

He moved behind her and bent to kiss her neck lightly. 'You are a princess,' he told her, 'just as you are.'

The ache began to build in her heart again.

Marc had rented a Land Rover, and somehow

acquired a picnic lunch packed in a hamper and stored in the back. They drove along the white coral streets, and stopped before particularly picturesque shop fronts or quaint stone houses, and Megan was never aware of posing for him. He walked along with her and pointed out the sites or told amusing stories, and occasionally, without her knowing it, began to click the shutter of his camera.

'Did you know,' he told her, 'that all the engineers had to do to build these gorgeous coral streets was to sweep away the earth on top of them? The entire island is nothing but limestone so soft you can crumple it in your hand, but after a period of time it hardens enough to support all the traffic these roads get year after year.'

'I love the carriages,' she commented. 'I wish they'd kept cars off the island the way it used to be. The horses and carriages and even the bicycles are so much more romantic.'

'Which would you prefer?' he asked her. 'Tell me your choice and we'll take it.'

'Oh,' she exclaimed, 'let's ride in an open carriage! I've always wanted to!'

And so they did. Megan, as excited as a child, turned this way and that as Marc pointed out various attractions and curiosities, and he continued to click the shutter unobserved.

Barefoot, they climbed on one of the coral reefs, and the surf splashed her legs and the wind pasted her dress to her slim body as she stood against the background of nature-carved stones, looking out breathlessly over the sea. Marc could not resist the image, and backed away from her, exclaiming in delight as he captured it on film. Afterwards, they unpacked their lunch beneath the shelter of a dune and feasted on roast beef and Burgundy, french bread and cheese.

Afterwards, she stretched out on the blanket and he lay beside her, propped up on one elbow, watching her. His camera lay forgotten at his side. It was the same blissful contentment Megan had experienced the morning before, and the events between that time and this seemed not to have happened at all. So this is what happened to the modern girl, she thought wryly. She's fallen head over heels in love with a man who drags her out of bars and locks her in rooms, tells her how to dress and wear her make-up, orders her meals for her and lectures her on morality ... And, she realised wistfully, she loved every minute of it.

And then he said, 'Tell me something, Megan.' She looked at him. 'What would your mother say if she knew?'

'Knew what?'

'What your real purpose for taking this vacation was.'

Her spirits plummeted. The last thing any girl wants to be reminded of when her thoughts take a romantic turn towards the man she loves is her mother. And Marc had effectively reminded her as well that, despite the wonderful morning they had just spent, despite what had passed between them last night in his bedroom, he still only thought of her as a wayward child to be protected.

She shrugged and looked away. 'She wouldn't approve, of course. If she knew.'

'But she will know,' he assured her.

Megan stared at him.

'Mothers always know,' he replied sagely, and drew her to her feet. His mood lightened suddenly. 'There's one more place I want to take you,' he said.

Megan drew in her breath when it first came into view. Along the side of the winding road, for miles and miles as far as the eye could see, stretched a field of pure white Easter lilies, nodding and whispering gently in the breeze. Their sweet, intoxicating scent reached them even through the open windows of the car. 'Oh!' she gasped, twisting in her seat to take it in all at once. 'I've never seen anything so beautiful!'

'They grow them here for export,' he told her. He brought the car around a bend and parked it on the kerb, out of the way of passing traffic, then he grabbed his camera and took her hand. 'Come on!'

The sweet perfume intermingled with the salt air was almost dizzying as he led her into the field, stepping carefully between the rows. The magnificent lilies stroked her ankles and her calves with their velvety softness, and she bent to inhale the scent, transported upon the field of beauty.

'This is you, darling,' Marc said softly, shutter clicking. 'This is where you belong ... fresh, innocent, but somehow other-worldly ... I shall treasure the memory of you at home among the lilies.'

The gentle breeze moulded the almost-transparent material of her dress against her as she walked, outlining the slender shape of her legs and hips. She laughed out loud in the delight with the beauty of it all, and stretched her hands overhead to embrace the sky and the eternal white carpet of lilies and even the little stone church in the distance, then she twirled around and around, growing dizzy with laughter.

Marc put aside his camera and ran towards her, catching her around the waist before she knew it and lifting her high overhead. She held on to his shoulders and squealed in protest, and he twirled her around, her skirt flying above her knees while the field and the sky turned into one kaleidoscopic blur of blue and white with the sparkling crystal blue of his laughing eyes at the centre. Countless lilies were crushed beneath his feet and she cried, 'Stop it—put me down—look at what you're doing to the flowers!'

'I'll buy the whole field!' he exclaimed, but he set her on her feet, laughing as she reeled against him dizzily, and then he began to tickle her.

'Oh, no—oh, don't——' she shrieked, and broke away, running across the field, and the stalks of lilies released their last sweet perfume before they bent to her careless steps.

He caught her about the waist, and as she struggled, choking with laughter and mock squeals of protest, lowered her gently to the soft bed of fragrant flowers. His mouth covered her last laughing shrieks.

She welcomed him joyfully, encircling his neck with her arms, melting into his presence with an instinctive, dizzying response. His hand moved to cup her breast, and his thumb gently explored the nipple through the thin material. Megan was breathless as he began to plant light kisses all over her hot face, murmuring, 'You're beautiful, my love ... my own love ... if only you knew how devastating you really are!'

His fingers began to unhurriedly work the cloth-covered buttons on her bodice, and it seemed she no longer breathed at all as he pushed the material aside to expose her breasts, bending to kiss each one in turn, gently, lovingly. Then, caressing her sensitive flesh tenderly with both hands, he lifted his face and looked into her eyes earnestly. 'I want,' he whispered, 'to make love you, here, amidst the flowers ...'

The small sound that caught in her throat was like a sob of pleasure, and swiftly Marc's mouth was upon hers again, insistently, urgently, his passion flaming into hers with a force that swept aside all but their consuming need for one another. His hands slipped aside to caress her bare back as he pressed her closer, crushed against the demanding rhythm of his heart, and she was lost ...

Then he released her abruptly. It was so sudden that not even a gasp escaped her until he sat up, turning away from her with one elbow propped up on his knee, grinding his forehead into his fist. His shoulders were square and hard with tension, and Megan could hear his slow, deliberate breathing above the whisper of the lilies.

She began to shiver. She felt bereft, betrayed, and aching with emptiness as she drew the two pieces of her dress across her exposed breasts with shaking fingers.

After a moment Marc said hoarsely, not turning around, 'Lord, child, I'm only human!'

She whispered tremulously, 'Marc...' She did not want it to end like this, uncertain, unhappy, unfulfilled. The aroma of the lilies suddenly seemed much too sweet.

'But then,' he added softly, releasing a breath, 'you'll make fools of us all.' His voice sounded calmer now, more in control. He turned to her, and there was a small, gentle smile on his lips, although it did not reach his eyes. 'And you,' he finished, barely above a whisper, 'are so unwise.'

Megan dropped her eyes miserably and began to fumble with the buttons of her bodice. In a moment his strong, assured fingers took over the task. 'Never,' he told her with a slight touch of wry humour to his tone, 'allow a man to choose a dress for you. You'll find he invariably selects one that opens down the front.'

And then he pulled her gently to her feet. She still could not look at him, and he gently tilted her face upwards with both his hands. There was not a trace of mirth in his expression now.

'Go home, Megan,' he told her soberly. 'Marry your dull George and live in your house in the suburbs and raise your two-point-two American children. It's the only course of safety I can promise you.'

Then he took her arm and led her slowly out of the field. Once he paused and broke off a single lily to place in her hair. That night Megan wrapped it carefully in tissue and pressed it beneath the heavy doorstop in her room. She knew that when she did return home, it would be all she would have of him.

CHAPTER SEVEN

MEGAN was afraid she would not hear from Marc again. She was not exactly certain how that terrible dread originated, but she suspected it might have been in his eyes when he had gently kissed her cheek as he left her at her door the evening before. He no longer trusted himself with her, and while that knowledge should have made her exultant, it in fact only plunged her into the darkest despair. For perhaps, by awakening passion in her, Marc had also discovered that she was no different from any other woman he had wooed and conquered.

She was breathlessly surprised when he called her the next morning, but she was not very surprised when he went on to make his excuses. 'I'll be working like mad the next few days trying to wrap this thing up, love,' he told her. 'I'm afraid that won't leave me much time for recreation.'

'Sure,' she responded, trying to sound nonchalant and mature. 'I understand.'

'What will you do with yourself without my charming company?'

'Don't worry,' she responded tiredly, 'I won't go throwing myself at any sex-starved men behind your back. Your commission as a knight in shining armour has just expired.'

He hesitated. 'What's that supposed to mean?'

'It means,' she replied tightly, 'that I don't need

a chaperone. I'm trying to make this easy for you, Marc. You don't have to put yourself out any more keeping an eye on me. I was getting a little tired of it, anyway.' She hung up the phone.

She expected it to ring again immediately, but it did not. She expected it to ring every minute of the day for the next forty-eight hours. Finally staring at it and willing it to ring became such an absorption that she had to leave her bungalow, spending most of her time walking along the edge of the surf or lying in the sun or lackadaisically exploring the souvenir shops in town. She stopped taking her meals at the hotel, afraid that if Marc saw her there he would only think she was lonely for him and was hoping to bump into him.

For of course he was right. She would go home to George and live out the rest of her dull, unsophisticated life in a town whose population was less than five thousand, she would be a dutiful wife and mother, and she would never know any other lover than her husband.

She had taken this trip to assert her identity, but in fact she had found out more about herself than she really wanted to. She was not designed to be a modern girl. She was designed with an old-fashioned heart that committed itself completely to one man . . . she loved not wisely but too well.

And she had fallen in love with the one man with whom a future was impossible, who had made it clear he would never think of her as anything more than a troublesome child. Even his display of passion for her meant nothing—it was an instinctive response which only served to irritate him, for Marc did not believe she was mature enough to receive him as a real woman receives a lover. Or perhaps it was something even simpler . . . jaded by the smart, sophisticated set in which he travelled, he had played out a fantasy with her, but soon saw the inconvenience of being encumbered with a foolish young virgin.

She only knew that she wanted to spend the rest of her life with him, but if one night was all he offered, she would have taken it gladly . . . if he had offered.

The days she had left here in the islands were slipping away, and she was losing them in misery over Marc. How typical her behaviour was of the very type of woman she was trying not to be! Deprived of her man, she was helpless and at a loose end, unable even to entertain herself. How Marc would laugh if he could see her now!

She decided to prove him—and herself—wrong. She *did* know what to do with herself when he was not around. She had come to the islands to assert her independence, and that she would do—though not, however, in so daring a way as picking up a man at the bar. Harbour tours departed every hour, and she found herself climbing on to the boat with ten or twelve other tourists, determining to enjoy herself.

There were benches arranged beneath the brightly striped awning on the gay little boat, and most of the passengers preferred to sit. A few stood at the rail, and Megan was one of them, leaning over and watching the arrow of frothy blue-green water disappear behind them. The motion of the boat and the hypnotic path it cut through the water was soothing, and she relaxed, drifting for a moment free of thoughts of Marc. She jumped when she felt a hand on her shoulder.

'Not seasick, are you?'

The young man who spoke was sandy-haired and pleasantly tanned, wearing white shorts and a pale yellow shirt. He had an open, nice-looking face.

Megan laughed. 'No, not at all. I guess I was leaning over a little far, though.'

'I thought we were going to have to throw you a raft,' he grinned. He leaned his arms on the rail beside her, still smiling pleasantly. 'Where are you from?'

'Maryland,' she told him.

'That's not far from where I live,' he responded, pleased. 'Delaware.' He extended his hand. 'How do you do, Maryland?'

She laughed and shook his offered hand. 'Very well, thank you, Delaware.'

'How do you like the islands?' he asked, when their mirth had passed. 'Oh,' she sighed, leaning again on the rail and gazing back at the shoreline, 'they're beautiful, aren't they? Paradise, just like the travel brochure said.'

'They are nice,' he agreed. 'But there's no place like home.'

Megan was a little homesick herself, though she would not admit it, and it was nice to talk to someone from her part of the country. He was the only one she had ever met who actually knew—or claimed to know—where Apple Corners was. They spent the entire cruise chatting like two old friends, and when the little boat pulled into the harbour again, she wondered whether he would ask to take her out. She wondered what she would say if he did. She thought about Marc and she wondered if this was what he would term a 'pick-up'. But how else did a modern girl meet men? And the only person she knew who had been picked up recently was herself, by Marc! She thought she would agree to see Delaware again, if he asked.

As they disembarked, he kept his hand lightly on her elbow to guide her through the crowd, and he said, 'Listen, if you're not busy the rest of the evening . . .'

She hesitated. The trouble was, she did not really *want* to go out with anyone but Marc. But she couldn't continue to mourn over Marc, he cared nothing about her and never would . . .

'I mean,' he continued, 'my hotel isn't far from here, we could grab a bottle of wine.'

She stared at him, not quite believing. 'What?'

He grinned. 'Okay, forget the wine.' His arm slid around her waist, drawing her to him firmly, and it was a singularly unpleasant sensation.

Megan wiggled out of his embrace. 'What,' she demanded incredulously, 'are you suggesting?'

'Ah, come on, baby,' he drawled. His grin was no longer attractive, and neither were his eyes as they raked her hotly up and down. 'You know the score. We're both grown up people here, you're not a bad-looking chick and you weren't exactly ready to push me overboard a minute ago. So why waste time with games? Let's get it on, honey.'

She gasped and pushed away from him. 'Get away from me!' she exclaimed, and turned to flee.

'Hey, what is this?' she heard him call angrily after her. 'What are you—some kind of square, or something?'

She pushed her way blindly through the crowd, her face on fire, every muscle in her body quivering with outrage.

'This is the twentieth century, baby!'

Megan ran out on to the kerb and hailed a cab.

In other circumstances it would have almost been amusing, but Megan was in no mood to laugh. She tried to calm herself on the way back to her bungalow, but every time she thought about it her cheeks would burn again and her stomach would churn. So you met one creep, she told herself sternly, it's nothing to fly to pieces about . . . No, make that two creeps. She remembered the man in the bar who hadn't even bothered to take off his wedding ring. And where was her gallant knight when she needed him? Despair swept her. She felt dirty and cheap and deeply, horribly ashamed. If this was what modern life was all about, she knew for certain now she was not meant for it. Marc had been right all along.

The telephone was ringing when she unlocked her door. Still a little shaken, she hesitated for a moment before going to answer it.

'Megan!' Marc's voice sounded anxious. 'I've been calling you all afternoon! Where have you been?'

Relief washed over her and she sank weakly to the bed. 'Just out,' was all she could manage to reply. It was so good to hear his voice . . . like coming home.

'Darling, are you all right?' he demanded. 'You sound upset.'

'No,' she answered, strength gradually returning to her voice. 'I'm fine.' One day she might tell him about what had happened, but not now, not tonight. She couldn't stand any lectures tonight.

There was a short pause, then he said, 'Well, I'm finished here. I just put my girls on a plane and officially started my holiday. Would you like to celebrate with me tonight?'

'I'd love to,' she replied, warmth seeping through her.

'Fine. Why don't you come on over and we'll grab a bite downstairs, then go somewhere quiet and dark and relax for a while. I'm just going to hop in the shower, so if I don't answer your knock come on in.'

'All right, that sounds fine.'

'See you in a few minutes, love.'

'See you!'

She hung up the phone slowly, smiling secretly and foolishly to herself.

She changed her clothes quickly and ran a brush through her hair. He *had* stayed, after all, and the next days belonged exclusively to them. He hadn't been simply making excuses not to see her, he had really been working, and now he had called and everything was going to be all right again. She hurried down the path to the hotel.

There was no response to her loud knock, so, as he had instructed, she let herself in. 'Marc!' she called. 'I'm here!'

Olivette Carlisle came from the bedroom. 'Hello, Megan,' she said.

Megan stared at her, feeling something cold and unpleasant begin to slip around her heart. Marc had said he had put the models on a plane, so what was she doing here, wearing only a pair of silk lounging pyjamas and a chiffon robe, coming out of Marc's bedroom . . .

As though reading her thoughts, Olivette smiled enigmatically. 'I was hoping we would get another chance to chat, dear,' she said. 'How fortunate you dropped by.'

'Marc . . .' began Megan, and then made a stern effort to gather her composure. 'Marc was expecting me,' she told her. 'Where is he?'

Olivette lifted a cool eyebrow. 'Was he? He didn't mention it to me.' She lifted her elegant shoulders casually. 'Perhaps he wanted another session with you. I don't believe the last batch of photos turned out at all the way he expected.' The slight arch of her eyebrow was both intriguing and somehow a little frightening as she invited, 'Come along, dear, I'll show you what I mean.'

The old line from a nursery rhyme ran irrationally through Megan's head: *Come into my parlour, said the spider to the fly* . . . But she followed her helplessly into the bedroom.

The scene was in some ways worse than she had expected, in some ways no more. The bedcovers were wildly tangled, both pillows rumpled. There were two glasses and a half-finished bottle of wine on the night-table. Marc's clothes lay scattered on the floor, as though he had flung them off in impatience. Confusion and hurt rampaged through her, but mostly confusion. Had Marc called her before he had got into bed with this woman, or after? And *why*?

Olivette watched the painful emotions cross Megan's face with a vague look of satisfaction, and then she turned casually to a selection of glossy photographs which were scattered across the desk. 'Come here, dear,' she said. 'Have a look at these.'

Megan crossed the room on numb legs, trying very hard not to give the other woman the satisfaction of knowing what damage she had wreaked in Megan's heart. She saw that the photographs were all of her, but it took a moment for her to bring her scattered senses together enough to examine them closely. And then she knew immediately why Olivette had shown them to her.

Several were the face shots Marc had taken on their last indoor session . . . the day when she had broken down before him and he had sent her home early. The others were the ones he had taken on their excursion about the island . . . on the streets, in the carriage, on the reef, in the lily field. And in every one of them was a girl who wore her heart in her eyes, looking with loving adoration toward the camera . . . or the man behind it.

'These,' said Olivette, flicking one uninterestedly with a long, well-manicured fingernail, 'as any blind man can see, were taken of a young woman in love. Very unwise of you, my dear,' she told her in a bored tone, 'as I tried to warn you the other day. Marc finds such things very off-putting.'

Megan choked, 'Marc—has seen these?'

'But of course. He was rather amused, I must say, but then it's not an unusual thing for him to encounter. I needn't tell you how irresistible he is.'

A twisting pain throbbed within Megan's heart. Then he knew! Having seen these photographs how could he not know that his foolish little protégée had fallen heedlessly in love with him . . . and he was laughing, just as she had feared he would. She had never wanted him to know! She could have borne it, even though he would never love her back, she could have kept her love for him safe and undefiled, but now he knew and what could she expect from him but amusement? It was too much—too much for her to stand.

'Of course I never took Marc to be a saint,' continued Olivette in the same bored tone. Megan wanted to run away, but she seemed to be rooted to the spot. 'There have been others, in and out— plenty of them, mostly foolish, ambitious young cats who get what they deserve. But it does disturb me,' she added with not a trace of compassion to her tone, 'to see a little innocent like you get washed away with the others. That's why I wanted to show you these—so that you can take charge of your life again before it's too late.'

Megan could say nothing. She could not even move. She only stood there and felt helpless tears of pain burn her eyes and she could not even lift her hand to wipe them away.

'I know,' continued Olivette airily, 'that right now you think *you* will be the one to change him, but believe me when I say that better women than you have tried. It always ends the same, and he comes back to me . . . do you know why? Because no one sinks her claws into Marc Campion. The minute they try he leaves them cold, and comes back to the one woman who can give him what he really needs.'

'That will do, Olivette.'

Marc stood at the door, wearing only a short

navy kimono and a towel about his neck. His hair
was still damp from the shower and there were
droplets of water on his face. His voice was cold,
but there was no expression in his eyes. None at
all.

He walked over to the telephone and lifted the
receiver. Megan was dimly aware of the other
woman, tense with shock and alarm, standing
beside her, but her only real thought was to flee, to
escape this room before she must face the pity in
his eyes.

'Gayle,' Marc said into the telephone, 'Miss
Carlisle seems to have somehow missed her plane.
Would you please make certain she's on the next
flight out? Oh,' he added casually, 'and make a
note that we won't be needing her services any
more. Ever.'

Megan heard Olivette's indignant gasp beside
her, she saw Marc calmly replace the receiver, but
she could not bear to look into his eyes. She
somehow found her strength and broke away,
running past him and into the other room; dimly
she heard him calling after her over the shrill
outrage in Olivette's voice, and then she was out of
the suite, running down the corridor through a
blur of tears.

She heard his voice again as she reached the
elevator, and then blessedly sealed it off with the
closing doors. She found her way out of the hotel
and on to the beach, and there, with no one to
witness but the sea, she sobbed out her grief.

She hid herself behind a rock pillar and
pressed herself into its shadow, drawing her
knees up to her chin and burying her face in her

skirts. It was there Marc found her some twenty minutes later.

He had not even taken time to dress, only to pull on a pair of shorts and an open shirt. He knelt beside her and placed a firm hand on her trembling shoulder. 'There now,' he said gently. 'That's enough.'

Megan tried desperately to control her sobs. She did not want his pity, she did not want his mockery, she only wanted to be left alone. She gulped and swallowed hard and by sheer force of will stopped the shudders that were racking her.

'The woman is mad,' he said calmly. 'She must have heard me on the telephone with you and plotted the whole thing. She wanted badly to hurt you, and it would appear she's done a fine job.'

There was a bitter note to his voice at the last, but it didn't matter now. The worst had happened, nothing could save it or intensify it. And there was no need for her to pretend any more. She lifted her head and looked at him. The muscles of his face were tight in the shadowy light, but his eyes were gentle. That gave her the courage to speak. 'You are,' she said thickly, 'having an affair with her.'

Marc shook his head slowly. 'We were lovers once,' he admitted. 'A long time ago. One of those brief, sophisticated, modern affairs that was over almost as soon as it began and ended with us parting friends—or at least I thought it did. Apparently Olivette had been plotting just this type of vengeance against me for a long time. I'm only sorry you had to be caught in the middle of a very nasty scene.'

Megan knew he was telling the truth, but

somehow that only made it worse. It didn't change the fact that their relationship must be irretrievably altered from this point on, and that she must face losing even his companionship because of it.

'Come on, darling,' he said gently, 'it was an ugly thing to happen, but it's over. Try to forget it. Don't sit on the wet sand, love, you'll catch cold.'

'No,' she gulped, but allowed him to pull her to her feet. 'It's not over.' She had to say it, even though she knew it was against every convention she had ever known. She had been brought up to believe that the woman always waited for the man to speak on such matters, and the girl she had once been would have quaked at the thought of tossing aside tradition and putting herself forward ... the old Megan would never have been so quick to wear her heart on her sleeve. But she was no longer that girl, she was only a woman in love, and she could not hide the truth, even if it meant losing whatever chance she had left with him—if, in fact, she had ever had any at all. 'You—you saw the pictures, and you heard what she said ...' She looked up at him, her eyes bright with tears and desperate with hurt, pleading with him to understand. 'It's true, Marc,' she whispered. 'I—I do love you!'

His eyes softened; he brought one hand up lightly to brush a tear off her cheek. 'Darling,' he exclaimed softly, 'why do you say that as though you're ashamed of it? Did you think I'd be angry to hear that I'm loved by someone as sweet and earnest as yourself? No, love ...' gently he bent and kissed her lips, 'I'm selfish enough to take all the love that's offered,' he added tenderly. 'And from you it's especially dear.'

Megan was confused, strangely relieved but at the same time empty and—yes, hurt. Those were not the words she had wanted to hear, but neither were they the paternal, superior words of reproach she had expected. Perhaps he was trying only not to hurt her more, but at least he was doing it in a gentle, thoughtful manner.

Marc slipped his arm about her shoulders. 'Let's walk for a while,' he suggested. 'Let's try to get a new start on our evening.'

Her new-found boldness suddenly disappeared, as though it had been completely used up in that one rash declaration. She did not have the strength to agree or disagree, and she let him lead her, as she had always done.

He talked of casual things, trying to give her a chance to recover herself and relax, and after a while he succeeded. After all, she still had his company, she still had a chance to be in his presence for however long they had left, and that was all that mattered . . . just being with him. She would not moon and cry or ever let him know how he was hurting her. She would not let him suspect how bleak her life would be without him. She would never again mention her feelings for him, if that was the way he wanted it, and for tonight, it was enough that they were together.

The sea seemed a little choppy tonight, and in the far distance the moon illuminated a string of purplish thunderheads. 'I wonder if we will get any rain,' commented Marc after a time.

'The weather has been almost too good to be true,' Megan answered, feeling foolish for discussing the weather when her heart was breaking. 'It would be a shame if it rained on my last few days here.'

'How much longer do you have?' he asked.

She answered, 'Five days.' And only five days before they would go their separate ways and her world would end . . . if even that long.

They had wandered to the beach in front of her bungalow, and Marc paused. 'We should get some dinner,' he said.

'I—I'm not very hungry,' she admitted.

'Would you like to be alone?'

'No,' she said quickly, and looked at him. She added in a more equable tone, 'That is, it's early yet . . .'

He bent his head suddenly and kissed her. It was a tender, sweet, and gentle kiss, and it was over too soon. When he lifted his face his eyes were very sober, and she looked into them in confusion.

'Megan,' he said quietly, 'do you really think you're ready for a summer romance?'

She began to shiver, searching his face. She whispered, 'Yes.'

He slipped his arm about her shoulders. 'Let's go inside, then.'

CHAPTER EIGHT

MEGAN'S legs were strangely weak as Marc led her up the path. Her heart was choking off her breath and she felt a little dizzy, from trepidation as well as excitement. As though sensing her feelings, Marc paused and placed a light kiss on her forehead. 'Frightened?' he asked softly.

She looked at him. Her eyes were wide and her lips parted breathlessly. 'A—a little,' she whispered.

His lips curved into a gentle, tender smile. 'Will you change your mind once we're inside?' His words were light, but there was a husky timbre of passion in his tone which caused her to shiver.

'N-no,' she whispered. Because she loved him, and if one night were all he offered, she would take it gladly.

And then, incredibly, a shadow stirred near her door and separated into a human form in the bright moonlight. 'Hello, Megan,' it said.

Megan smothered a little cry and drew closer to Marc. She stared for a long time, not believing her eyes. She felt Marc's arm tense about her shoulders.

'G-George!' she gasped.

He stepped forward. 'Surprised?'

Marc's arm gradually relaxed about her, she felt him release a breath that sounded both resigned and amused. Still, it took her another moment before she could regain herself sufficiently to reply, weakly, 'Y-yes!'

Marc stepped forward quickly and extended his hand. 'I'm Marc Campion. Megan has mentioned you often.'

George shook his hand pleasantly. 'George Elsing. Glad to know you.'

'Marc is a photographer,' offered Megan hastily. 'A professional photographer. He's been letting me pose for him—model, I mean. Magazines and stuff, fashion shows.'

She was aware her near-incoherence was amusing Marc greatly, but George appeared impressed. 'Is that right? I always did know Megan was an enterprising woman,' he added with a note of approval, 'and leave it to her to find a way to work on her vacation!'

Megan burst out, 'What in the world are you *doing* here, George?'

'Well, I . . .'

'Megan,' interrupted Marc, 'I'm sure your friend has had a long trip and doesn't want to stand about in the night air bringing you up to date. Will you allow me,' he offered to George, 'to take you both to dinner at the hotel?'

George beamed. Generosity was not one of his strong points, and a free meal was always welcome. 'Well, that's good of you. I took a late flight and they didn't serve anything but peanuts . . .'

Megan still could not believe as they walked, an amicable threesome, toward the hotel. George, of all people! It was worse than seeing a ghost! For George to spend the money on a flight!

'Is anything wrong at home?' she demanded suddenly, a terrible fear gripping her. It was the only explanation she could think of.

'Oh no,' he assured her easily. 'It's just that—well, you knew I had a few days off this week, and I thought, why not fly down and see what Megan's up to? I knew you must be bored out of your mind by now,' he confided, 'but were just too proud to give it up and come home. So I thought I'd make it a little easier for you, and get in some sun myself. Your parents don't know I'm here,' he added to her. 'So it might be best not to mention it.'

Megan caught a giggle just in time. It was the closest thing to 'daring' George had ever done in his life. 'But,' she protested, 'to go to such expense, for just a few days! That's not like you, George.'

Now warming to his favourite topic he agreed, 'It's ridiculous, what they charge for airline tickets these days! And the hotel—it's nice, granted, but why pay all that money for a place to sleep? I mean, no one stays in their room on vacation, right? All you do is sleep, and what do you care how nice the room is then?'

'It's frightful,' agreed Marc, and George looked smug. 'But then one hasn't a great deal of choice, so they have us, as the term goes, over a barrel. I shouldn't be a bit surprised if it weren't all some sort of conspiracy.'

Megan glanced at him sharply, but his face was blandly sincere.

'Exactly!' agreed George enthusiastically. 'Of course I tried to tell Megan it was all a giant rip-off, but she was determined to spend her life's savings on a two-week vacation. Can you imagine that? I say, I work too hard for my money to go throwing it away at the drop of a hat!'

'Well,' agreed Marc sagely, 'we can't expect women to have any sense about money; that's what makes them women.'

Megan stared at him. She couldn't believe this!

The two men continued to chat amicably and Megan remained speechless with amazement. The events of the day had been bad enough, but now her evening was turned topsy-turvy, and she was having difficulty adjusting to the incredible turn of events. And Marc—what had got into him? Only moments ago he had been ready to take her to his bed, and now he was chatting with every show of amiability with the man who should have been his rival. What kind of man was he?

As they were seated, Megan had her first opportunity to actually observe the two of them, and, as she had suspected he would, George suffered badly by comparison. He was a pleasant-enough looking man under ordinary circumstances, with brown hair and eyes and a very ordinary face. But he was at least twenty pounds lighter and three inches shorter than Marc, next to Marc's vibrant tan his skin looked pasty, and he had a slight paunch about his middle Megan had never noticed before. Why, she thought, he'll be fat in ten years!

But the physical differences, clear as they were, were not the most remarkable. George had a tense, wound-up look about him that was perpetual. He moved in quick, jerky motions and had a habit of constantly darting his eyes about when he was talking—a shifty look, thought Megan. She had never noticed that before, either. Marc's easy, relaxed manner and quiet strength made George look like a schoolboy.

She knew she was being disloyal, but she coudn't help it. She was fond of George, they had been friends since grade school, and she knew and had accepted all his weaknesses. If she had never met Marc, she possibly would have been perfectly satisfied with him as a husband ... if she had never met Marc.

Over the traditional steak and baked potato, Marc dropped the bombshell. 'Megan tells me you two are to be married,' he commented casually.

Megan stared at him. George brought his napkin casually to his lips and replied, 'Well, yes, eventually, of course. We've had to put it off for a while because after all, a man can't just jump into marriage without building a comfortable nest, you know.'

'Quite right,' agreed Marc. 'You want your wife to be at home taking care of the children, not worrying about how to make ends meet.'

'But I want to work!' Megan objected. She turned to George. 'We've discussed that, and——'

'Now, now!' George patted her hand in an irritatingly soothing gesture. 'That's just another one of your silly notions you'll get over soon enough once we're married. Liberated women!' he turned to Marc for support. 'Have you ever heard of anything so ridiculous?'

'Never,' agreed Marc heartily. 'Women were designed to be wives and mothers, and whenever they try to be anything else, they only find themselves in trouble.'

Megan felt as though she were in the middle of a nightmare. 'I don't believe this!' she exclaimed. 'I've never heard such a bunch of garbled logic in my life! I——'

'Now, Megan, don't fly into one of your tantrums,' said George. 'You just wait until you hear my surprise and you'll cheer up soon enough.'

Megan felt a dread seeping over her, mingled with confusion. 'Surprise?' she parroted.

George sipped his coffee, pausing for effect. 'Do you remember that house out on Elkwood? The one you've always liked?'

Remember it? She had dreamed about it for years, a gorgeous Georgian brick structure with four fireplaces and a spiral staircase and two genuine stained-glass portals and azalea bushes that almost reached the second storey . . . the dread that was closing in about her heart suddenly intensified.

'Well,' added George casually, 'it just went on the market last week. The owner is being transferred, so I practically got it for a song. I've already made arrangements with the bank . . .'

The rest of his speech washed over her. He had done it! He had bought the house. *Her* house. Their house. The reality of Apple Corners came closing in on her, smothering the exotic beauty of the islands and her dreams of independence.

She looked up to catch Marc watching her intensely. He shifted his gaze abruptly, though, and offered with every appearance of goodwill, 'It sounds as though congratulations are in order.'

'Yes,' agreed George broadly, 'they are.' He turned to Megan. 'Your mother is already planning the engagement party, and a whole string of showers. I figure we should be able to be married by the end of the summer. By that time the house will be ready to move in to, and you can give Dr Brandon plenty of notice . . .'

'Yes,' agreed Megan dazedly, 'I suppose so.'

Marc signalled for the check and said genially, 'Well, I know you two have a lot to talk about. I think I'll call it an early night, myself.' He signed the check and offered his hand to George, smiling warmly. 'Again, congratulations. Megan,' he glanced at her, and if there were anything other than good will in his eyes he hid it effectively. 'Much happiness.'

She was too numb to reply.

He rose, and had taken a step away before he suddenly turned back, lifting a finger as though he had suddenly recalled something. 'Oh, Megan,' he said, 'don't forget to collect your dress from my room. You left it there the other night, remember?'

Megan gaped at him, but his expression remained bland.

For a moment George frowned. 'Your dress?' he echoed. Then his brow cleared. 'Oh, that's right,' he said, and turned back to his coffee. 'You were modelling.'

'Oh, no,' corrected Marc easily. 'We weren't modelling *that* night.' He smiled at her. 'Were we, Megan?'

What was he trying to do? she wondered wildly. Her cheeks grew hot and she could not look at George, but she stammered, 'I—I don't want it. It was torn, anyway.' Then she could have bitten her tongue. What *would* George think? Probably only the truth.

But George only replied mildly, 'Nonsense, Megan. It can be mended. Waste not, want not. Now that you're about to be a married woman, you've got to learn to be a little more thrifty.'

There was an odd expression on Marc's face, but he only said pleasantly, 'Never mind, Megan, I'll bring it around in the morning. Goodnight, all.'

Megan was speechless and shaken as George finished his coffee in leisure, but he appeared not to notice. At last he said, 'Well, I'm a little tired myself, Megan—long trip, and all, you know. I'll walk you back to your cabin and then turn in early, I think.'

They walked back along the same moonlit path she and Marc had taken less than two hours ago, but now it was all changed. The purplish clouds in the distance no longer seemed romantic, but more threatening. There seemed to be fewer stars— probably, she thought with George's typical pragmatism, because of a high cloud cover.

George commented, 'Wasn't it more expensive to get a private cabin than a room in the hotel?'

'No,' she answered. 'As a matter of fact, it was a little cheaper. No maid service.'

'I wish I'd known that,' he mused. Then, more cheerfully, 'but I don't suppose it matters, for two nights.'

'Oh,' answered Megan, for some reason feeling her spirits rise. 'You're not staying?'

'Now, you know I have to be back at work on

Monday,' he explained impatiently. 'I've already
made reservations for us on the eight o'clock
flight . . .'

'Us?' She stopped a few feet away from her
door, and turned to him. *Us?'* she repeated
incredulously.

'Well, of course you'll come back with me.
You're getting married in a couple of months, you
haven't time to be gallivanting around on an
island vacation——'

'What?' The tension of the entire terrible night
exploded all at once. She turned on him like a little
fury. 'This is *my* vacation, the only one I've had in
three years, I've worked hard for it and saved for
it, and I intend to enjoy it! You can't come
strolling in here and tell me to go home! We're not
married yet!' she spat.

'Megan!' he protested in alarm. 'Lower your
voice!' Then, 'Be reasonable, will you? What do
you want to stay here for? I was just giving you a
chance to get out of it gracefully—that's the only
reason I came down here. That,' he added, 'and to
tell you about the house.'

'You didn't even *ask* me before you went out
and bought the house!' Megan exclaimed. 'Don't
you think we should have discussed it first?'

George looked puzzled and hurt. 'But it's what
you've always wanted. I thought you would be
pleased.'

She sighed, emotion draining out of her into
fatigue. She didn't want to hurt him. And he had
only done what he thought she wanted . . . he had
meant well. 'I'm sorry, George,' she said, 'I didn't
mean to fly at you. It *was* sweet of you to buy the

house, and it is what I've always wanted, it's just—well, I guess I'm a little shocked to see you.'

He smiled indulgently. 'That's okay,' he said. 'I guess I did kind of sweep you off your feet.'

The thought of George sweeping anyone off her feet was absurd, and its very absurdity made her feel a little maternal towards him. She smiled at him.

'You get some rest, now,' he told her, and kissed her lightly on the lips. 'I'll see you tomorrow, and you can show me what's so great about this island at fifty dollars a day.'

Megan watched him go with something like pity in her eyes. Because George would never understand, not in a million years.

George was stable and secure and eligible by the standards of a place such as Apple Corners. He had a good position with a Baltimore firm and he was rising rapidly. He worked hard and earnestly. If he was a little cheap, it was only because he wanted the best for his family. If he lacked imagination, it was only because he believed in keeping his feet firmly on the ground. He would be a good husband, a good provider, a good father. She could hardly ask for more. She had never really even had a choice.

She *was* fond of George, that was true enough. They had always got along well. And wasn't there an old saying about the three loves in a woman's life: her first love, her great love, and the love she marries. George had been the first and would probably be the last, but it would be Marc who haunted her secret dreams for the rest of her life.

Slow, sluggish tears slipped from beneath her

closed eyes as she turned over in bed and tried to go to sleep. Sleep was a long time coming.

The next day dawned grey and overcast, and somehow George made her feel guilty about that. 'I wish we could get a flight out today,' he complained as they walked along the beach in front of her bungalow. 'There hardly seems to be any point in hanging around another day, with the weather like this.'

'A little rain isn't going to hurt you,' she told him. 'This is the first day it's been cloudy since I've been here—and George, I told you, I don't want to go home tomorrow. You go on and I'll be back on Friday, just like I planned. There's plenty of time to do all those things you seem to think I just *have* to do, and there's no reason in the world to spoil my vacation.'

An obstinate look brewed on his face. 'Spoil your——?'

But fortunately he was interrupted by a call from over her shoulder.

'Megan!' It was Marc's voice.

She turned and saw him standing near her bungalow, waving. She returned his wave gladly and she and George started towards him.

'I've brought your dress,' he told her as they reached him. And there it was, the wicked monstrosity of fuchsia, glittering in the muted light as he passed it to her loosely. 'I had a feeling you might be leaving earlier than you planned, and I knew you wouldn't want to forget this.'

'Th-thank you,' she choked, and bundled it quickly under her arm, trying to compress it into invisibility.

'As a matter of fact,' George told him, 'you're right. We've got a flight out in the morning. Megan's anxious to get home,' he added, and Megan glared at him, astounded. 'You know how a girl is about her wedding.'

'Of course,' smiled Marc, and just as Megan began to sputter angrily a few large drops of rain spattered on her bare arm.

George looked up at the sky in disgust. 'Oh, lord, here it comes!' He glanced at Megan. 'I'm going back to the hotel before I get soaked. You'd better get busy packing.'

He started quickly away, and then turned back, adding, 'If this rain keeps up there's no point in our going out tonight. I'll come by for you about seven in the morning.'

He broke into a run as the rain began to increase to an irregular patter. Megan only stared after him, indignant and incredulous, and, because she felt Marc's eyes on her, embarrassed.

She felt certain he would make some remark about independent women, but all he did was enquire casually, 'Are you in the habit of leaving your personal garments in strange men's hotel rooms?'

Megan stared at him, confused and impatient. The rain began to pelt on to her curls. 'I don't know what you're talking about.'

He shrugged. 'Your young man didn't seem too upset to hear about it.'

'Oh,' she dismissed it impatiently, 'that's just George. He never gets upset about anything.'

'He seems nice enough.'

She brushed a fat, cold raindrop off her

shoulder and looked up at him, her despair and her anger with George combining to make her retort sharply, 'I don't need your approval, thank you!'

'I doubt whether my approval would make any difference to you at all,' he agreed. The rain was making the red streak in his hair glisten, and his eyes were as blue and bright as ever. Her heart ached. 'As I've already told you, Megan, you will forever bend your will to a man's. You were born to follow where he leads you. And now your solid, dependable George announces that you'll be on the morning flight for home, that you'll be married this summer, that you will move into your house on Elkwood and live happily ever after ... even though none of those things may be your first inclination, you will agree to them because you're used to doing so. You are not, my dear, an independent woman.'

'That's not true!' she cried indignantly. 'You don't know anything about it! I can make up my own mind, I——'

'Can you?' he queried politely. 'Well then, you think about this while you're deciding: Nice young ladies don't marry nice young men when they're already in love with someone else.'

Then, in the wake of her speechless astonishment, he turned on his heel and left.

Megan stared after him in astonishment and confusion.

The rain increased steadily throughout the afternoon, and the wind rose to fling curtains of water against her windowpanes and howl eerily about the eaves. What a horrible way to spend her last day here, cooped up inside by a rainstorm! She thought about what Marc had said and it made her angry. She was not a mindless female to be led around by the nose by any man who happened to come along! And this was *not* her last day here. She would stay and finish her vacation the way she had planned, and what did she care what either George or Marc thought about that? She still had a few weeks of independence left, and she would show them both she was not so easily subdued!

'Nice young ladies don't marry . . . when they're in love with another man.' What had Marc meant by that?

It disturbed her when she thought about that. Was he mocking her again, reminding her of how shamelessly she had confessed her love for him the night before and how quickly she appeared to have forgotten it when George showed up? Was he only pointing out again that she was too immature to make her own decisions, too foolish to know what she really wanted? But he had *wanted* her to marry George!

By six o'clock the rain had increased to such a force that she was afraid to even walk to the hotel for dinner. The greyish sea churned, flinging its brine high on the rocks, and gusts of wind shook the thin walls of the little bungalow. The pounding against the roof and the windows was deafening and ceaseless. Megan began to worry. Tropical storms could be fierce. Suppose the tide rose? Some of the breakers could get twenty feet high. Suppose . . .

At nine o'clock, the lights suddenly flickered and went out.

She had been standing at the window, peering through the sheets of rain and imagining that she saw the surf rising and hurtling across the breaker that separated the bungalow area from the beach. She cried out as she was suddenly plunged into blackness.

For a moment there was absolute panic. She was alone in the dark with a storm pounding about her, and she was terrified. She had never felt so isolated. Even the two bungalows next to hers were deserted, the young girls having gone home two days ago, the family having left this morning. Megan could no longer even see the dim lights of the hotel, although whether it was because the black-out had reached there as well, or because the rain was too heavy, she did not know. Her heart was pounding in her ears even over the din of the storm. She was trapped here alone in the dark with the rising surf threatening to sweep her away . . .

With a tremendous effort she took hold of herself. She took long, slow breaths, then fumbled her way back to the bed, bumping into furniture and biting back cries. She tried to tell herself not to worry. The wind had probably just knocked the line down; the lights would be on in a few minutes. Maybe they wouldn't even be on until morning, but there was nothing she could do about it. There was no danger. If there was any danger, someone from the hotel would come down to warn her . . . She would just have to relax and wait it out. With one final, calming breath, she made up her mind to do just that.

Anchoring herself to the bed, she reached across and fumbled on the small chest of drawers for her nightgown. There was no point in sitting up all night worrying about it. The lights were out and they might stay that way, so she might as well go to bed.

She changed into her nightgown in the dark and climbed into bed. But she did not sleep. She pulled the covers up round her ears and lay there, trying to drown out the sounds of the storm with the blankets, squeezing her eyes shut against the inky dark.

And then another sound shot through the din of the storm, causing her to sit bolt upright, her heart in her throat, staring sightlessly through the dark. It was the sound of pounding on her door, and a voice, dim and far away beneath the roar of the wind. 'Megan! Open the door!'

She stumbled out of bed and across the room, not feeling the pain as she bruised her shins and her toes, sobbing out loud in relief. She fumbled for the door handle and finally found it, flinging open the door on a gust of wind and a flood of rain, and then fell into his arms. 'Marc!' she gasped.

He closed the door quickly behind him as he encircled her tightly with his other arm. 'There, darling,' he murmured, 'it's all right. I knew you'd be frightened out of your wits. Look at you, you're trembling!'

She felt his strength beneath the slick wet substance of his raincoat and his cheek against hers, warm and rough despite the rain that still clung to it. Then he pushed her a little away. 'Hold on, now, you're getting wet. Let me get this thing off.'

'Don't leave me!' she gasped. 'I can't see you!'

'I've prepared for that,' he replied, but one hand held hers tightly as the other reached inside his coat. 'Candles! Let me light a match.'

The light flamed blindingly for a moment, then dimmed to a yellowish glow as he placed it to the candle. Blinking rapidly until her eyes adjusted to the new light, Megan finally made out his face. 'I lifted them off the dining room tables, but I don't think anyone will mind. I saw the hotel lights come on again just as I got here. Hold this, darling, and let me get out of this wet mac.'

She took the candle with a trembling hand while he shrugged out of the dripping black mackintosh and hung it near the door. 'Oh, Marc,' she whispered tremulously, 'you shouldn't have come out in this weather!' But she was *so* glad he had.

'You didn't look to me like the type of girl who would weather storms very well,' he told her.

Her fear swelled again. 'Marc . . .' she touched his arm unsteadily, 'you don't think—you don't think it will turn into a hurricane, do you?'

'No chance,' he replied with confidence. 'The weather bureau has already diagnosed this as nothing more than one of those annoying tropical storms that will blow out to sea by morning.' He took a handful of candles out of his pocket and dumped them on the table. 'It may take that long for the repair men to get to your power line, as well, so we'll make good use of these.' He lit two more and the room sprang into a cosy light. 'This reminds me of a three-day stretch I spent one time in the South Pacific,' he continued easily as he searched about the room for improvised candle holders. 'Now *that* part of the world has some storms, let me tell you! The surf broke at fifty feet and trees with trunks as big around as a good-sized automobile were carried through the air like toothpicks. But even that one didn't compare to the one I weathered on the Isle of Mango.'

Megan giggled. '*The Rime of the Ancient Mariner*,' she retorted. 'There's no such place as Mango.'

Marc grinned. 'And how would you know?'

'I know you're just trying to cheer me up.'

'Doing a good job?'

She smiled. 'Yes.'

'Excellent.' He took the candle from her and carried it to the night table. There was an ashtray there and he stuck the candle to it with melted wax. 'In bed, were you? The best place to be.' He grasped her hand and pulled her forward. 'In you go, love, and cover up tight.'

He helped her into bed and drew the covers over her. But she reached for his hand as he straightened up. 'Marc, you're not going, are you?'

He smiled down at her. 'Now, you really don't expect me to pass the night in one of those damnably hard chairs, do you?'

She dropped her eyes, her spirits sinking almost to the point they had been before he had arrived. 'N-no,' she admitted. 'I suppose not.' But she did not want to be left alone with the storm howling outside, any more than she wanted to think of him struggling back to the hotel in the worst of it.

He looked at her for a moment longer. 'That bed,' he said at last, 'appears to be adequate for two.'

Megan drew in her breath, a warm colour fanning her cheeks as she lifted her eyes to his questioningly.

Marc simply smiled gently and brushed her forehead with a kiss. 'I'm soaked to the skin, love. Let me get out of my wet things.'

She lay there, trembling with anticipation and disbelief and not a little fear, until he returned from the bathroom with a towel wrapped around his waist. He spread his clothes over chairs to dry, blowing out the candles as he went. Then he came over to her and blew out the last candle. He discarded the towel and she felt his nude body slip into bed beside her. He slipped an arm about her and drew her head on to his shoulder. She was trembling violently now.

He bent down to kiss her lips, gently and briefly, while his hand stroked her hair. 'Hush now, love,' he whispered. 'It's all right.'

This was what she wanted, she was sure of it. Then why should she feel so uncertain? How could being in bed with him now feel so right, so perfectly good, and yet at the same time so wrong?

She placed her hand on his chest. The thick mat of hair beneath her fingers was soft and springy, his skin was warm. She could feel his heartbeat, slow and steady. She whispered, trying to see his eyes in the dark, 'Marc . . .'

'Shh!' He bent again to kiss her, but this time on the cheek. Then he settled her head back on his shoulder. 'Go to sleep, Megan,' he said.

CHAPTER NINE

WHEN Megan stirred the next morning it seemed only natural, in her sleepy, dreamily-confused state, that she should find herself in Marc's arms. He brushed her eyelids lightly with his lips and whispered, 'Don't wake, love. I'm just going to take a shower.'

She murmured a drowsy assent and drifted off to sleep again.

It was no wonder she slept so heavily that morning; sleep had been a long time coming the night before. She had lain there for hours, every muscle in her body tense next to Marc's, listening to the storm rage and finally begin to die away, unable to believe that they were actually in bed together but only sleeping. She listened to his breathing grow heavy and relaxed, and she loved him more than ever. It was finally exhaustion that pushed her into a deep slumber.

A knocking on the door woke her again what seemed like only seconds later. She moaned and tried to ignore it, pulling a pillow over her head. But it was insistent, and finally she stumbled out of bed, disorientated and sleepy and remembering nothing.

She flung open the door, and George stood there. 'What are you doing?' he demanded. 'Don't tell me you overslept!'

Megan rubbed her eyes in the bright morning

light that spilled over the threshold, blinking and squinting at him. 'Wh-what?'

'It's past seven,' he told her impatiently, and stepped inside. 'We've got a plane to catch. Hurry up and get dressed!'

She stared at him as it slowly came back to her—but not soon enough.

She heard Marc's voice over her shoulder, 'Darling, have you got——'

She whirled helplessly as Marc came in from the bathroom, a towel wrapped around his waist, casually combing his still-damp hair. She seemed to stop breathing entirely as she looked back to George, and saw his eyes take in the entire scene at once—Megan's skimpy nightgown and sleep-dishevelled appearance, Marc's nakedness, the rumpled bed, the gutted candles, Marc's clothes arranged casually on the chairs.

Marc said cheerfully, 'Good morning, old man. Fine storm we had last night, wasn't it?'

George's face registered absolutely nothing at all. He simply said stiffly, 'Megan, I think we'd better talk about this at the hotel. I'll wait for you in the lobby.'

Megan sank weakly to a chair when he was gone, and Marc murmured, 'Talk about it? What the devil can he want to talk about? It seems perfectly obvious to me.'

She stared at him dazedly. 'Oh, Marc!' she gasped. 'He thinks—you and I—that we——'

'As well he should,' responded Marc, walking over to her, 'unless he's blind or stupid, and at first glance he seemed neither to me. Excuse me, poppet, I need my trousers.'

'But—but you don't understand!' she cried, jumping up in agitation as he attempted to tug his trousers off the chair on which she was sitting. 'I mean, he doesn't understand, he thinks——'

'Oh, I think he understands, well enough,' replied Marc enigmatically. 'And I must say I'm rather disappointed in the fellow.'

'D-disappointed!' stammered Megan, still not following him. 'What in the world do you mean? Don't you know——'

'I only know,' he told her, 'that if you were *my* girl, and I found you in bed with another man, I'd have laid the fellow flat and given you something to think about the rest of your life, too!'

'But—but he didn't find us in *bed* together—not actually——' Her confusion was mounting.

'He would have,' returned Marc shortly, and went back into the bathroom, 'if he'd showed up on time.'

For a moment she only stood there, staring after him, stunned. And then it gradually began to make sense.

'You——' she choked incredulously as he returned from the bathroom a moment later, 'You planned this! You heard him tell me he'd be by this morning, and you—you arranged it all, so that he would find us——!'

'My final and most brilliant object lesson,' he agreed, and pulled on his shirt. 'Although I can't take all the credit—the storm was most advantageous.'

Megan heard a rasping sound in her throat which was her outraged intake of breath. 'How—could you!' she choked. The beautiful memories of the night before suddenly dimmed and blackened. She had loved Marc so intensely . . . he had braved the storm for her, when George hadn't even given her a thought . . . he had lain beside her and comforted her . . . he had made her believe it was because he cared for her, but it had all only been a part of some cruel joke! It was all too horrible.

'But,' she cried, and the confusion was the worst part, 'you *wanted* me to marry George! You told me so! Why would you——?'

'But,' he replied, 'you didn't want to marry him. And let me tell you something, pet, if he'll have you after today, perhaps he deserves you. And if *you*'ll have *him* after his remarkably unchivalrous behaviour a moment ago, perhaps you're only getting what you deserve as well!'

'I was never going to marry George!' she cried, and for the first time she knew it was absolutely true. 'I could have told him so myself without your interference!'

'You never would have,' Marc told her, and sat on the bed to put on his shoes. 'You didn't until last night know *what* you wanted, and correct me if I'm wrong, but without my apparently unwelcome help you'd have gone on doing exactly as you've always done—following orders. Now, that's a very admirable trait, no doubt, and one I recommend highly in a woman, but in this case I couldn't help but feel you were following orders from the wrong man.'

'You——' she cried, hoarse with rage, '*you*—felt! How *dare* you! You've interfered in my life for the last time! You've gone too far!'

Marc looked at her, a slight frown furrowing his

own brow. 'Well,' he said, 'I should think you'd be grateful to me, instead of ranting and raving like a mad thing. I've just saved you from ruining both your lives——'

'You—*saved* me!' She choked on an hysterical laugh. 'I don't need your "saving", thank you! I can manage my own life, and I'm not telling you again—*stay out of it!* As a matter of fact, get out of my room—get out of my life—I don't *need* your kind of help!'

She was almost sobbing with rage and hurt, and as Marc passed her his face seemed rather cold. 'Well,' he said distantly, 'I suppose that's clear enough. Best of luck, then.'

'I'll marry George if I want to!' she cried.

'But you don't want to,' he reminded her coolly, and opened the door.

'I don't want to marry you, either!' she stormed, and wasn't even aware of having said the words until it was too late; hysteria had taken over.

He turned back with a slight lift of the eyebrow. 'I,' he replied, 'don't recall asking you.'

He closed the door.

Megan flung herself on the bed and beat the pillows and sobbed out her rage in a loud voice until she was spent.

She still had to meet George. She had to explain to him, somehow, make him understand ... Explain what? Make him understand what? He had interpreted the scene correctly, if not strictly. The only reason she *hadn't* made love with Marc was his self-control, not hers. The fact was, she had wanted to, and if the thought was as good as the deed then she was as guilty as George could suppose. She had never intended to marry George, not really, and it had been cruel of her not to tell him so before.

But maybe Marc was right. It was very possible that she might have allowed herself to wander into marriage with a man she did not love, simply because it was the expected thing, the correct thing, the easy thing to do. Easier, by far, than seeing the hurt disbelief on George's face when she told him. Easier than facing the reproaches from her mother, the sympathy from her girl friends, the cancelled parties and showers ...

She had come to the islands telling herself she was an independent woman, determined to prove the state of her own liberation ... but deep down inside she was still the same old-fashioned Megan Brown. She was old-fashioned enough to fall in love, deeply and irretrievably in love, with the first dashing, romantic figure that crossed her path. She was old-fashioned enough to want to belong to him completely and for ever ... and it was her very ideas of liberation that had now lost him to her.

Megan trudged to the hotel deep in dark despair. In one morning she had lost both the man she loved and the man she was going to marry. You've made a fine mess of your life, Megan Brown, she told herself bleakly. A fine mess.

George was waiting for her in the coffee shop. She slipped into the chair opposite him, miserable and too ashamed for a moment to look at him. Finally she had to break the oppressive silence, and she began, 'George, I'm s——'

'Megan,' he said abruptly, 'I think it's best if we

both forget what I saw this morning. I'm sure you have some perfectly logical explanation, but I would prefer you keep it to yourself. It's not really important.'

She stared at him. Did he really care for her so much that he was willing to trust her when all the evidence spoke to the contrary? For a moment her heart softened and flooded with warmth. George was a good man, he knew she would never try to deceive him—and that made her feel all the more guilty, for deceive him was exactly what she had tried to do. Yet he would forgive her in spite of that ...

'But George,' she insisted earnestly, 'I *do* have an explanation, and it's not at all what you think. I want to tell you——'

'I'd rather you didn't,' he said coldly. 'The important thing is that this marriage go on as planned, I think. It will save embarrassment all around.'

Megan stared at him. 'Embarrassment?'

'Yes,' he continued in the same flat, unemotional tone. 'The explanations to our friends, and relatives, the awkwardness ... And it may not have occurred to you, Megan, but I have a great deal of money tied up in that house, and it's a good investment. I really can't see the point in giving it all up now. I think it's best if we just forget all this happened and proceed as planned.'

'Yes,' she said softly, and dropped her eyes. 'I see.'

'So we're agreed?'

She looked at her hands, folded tightly on the

table, for a long time, then she looked up. 'I can't marry you, George,' she said.

His eyes widened incredulously. 'What? I just told you, what happened this morning doesn't matter——'

'It matters to me,' she said firmly. 'It matters, and I simply can't marry you.'

'But why?' he insisted. 'Why, all of a sudden——'

'Because I don't love you,' she told him gently, 'and you don't love me.'

'Of course I love you,' he defended uncomfortably.

She shook her head sadly. 'No, you don't. If you loved me, you would have made a good attempt to see that Marc didn't leave my bedroom alive this morning, and you wouldn't be sitting here now telling me that it doesn't matter.'

'I'm not a violent man,' he protested uncomfortably, 'you know that.'

She reached across the table and patted his hand gently. 'Yes, I know,' she said softly.

'Megan,' George insisted desperately, 'think what you're doing! What about all our plans? What about the house?'

She stood. 'I'm sorry, George,' she said. 'I really am.'

He glared up at her. 'Is that your final word?'

She nodded.

He glanced at his watch and swore under his breath. 'I'm going to miss my plane!' He grabbed up his ever-present raincoat and pushed past her. 'Don't come crawling back to me later, Megan,' he warned her. 'I gave you your chance. I'm going right home and put that house back on the market, and after that it will be too late!'

She nodded. 'I understand.'

He gave her one more dark look of impatience and disappointment, and then he hurried out the door.

More than anything in the world, Megan wanted to go upstairs to Marc right then. But she had ruined that, too. He would never forgive her for the way she had treated him this morning, and even if he did, it wouldn't matter. They had no future together. Marc Campion, internationally famous photographer, and plain old Megan Brown of Apple Corners, Maryland ... it was ridiculous! At most, they might have shared a few nights of passion together, and now she had spoiled even that. She had flung herself at his head once too often, he had mocked her for a child for the last time ... She could not face him now, knowing that even last night, as tender and as loving as she had taken it to be, was only a hoax. All she had ever meant to Marc was a foolish girl in need of protection, arousing the fatherly instinct in him. And now she had made it abundantly clear she no longer wanted even that ...

The worst was, of course, knowing that he was right. She *should* be grateful to him. But his final 'object lesson' had been too cruel. She simply could not face him again.

Back at her room, she called the airlines and discovered she could be on a three o'clock flight for home. There didn't seem to be much else to do, now. By the time she got home, George would have broken the news to her parents ... she wondered how much he would say. Could he be so spiteful as to tell them *why* their unofficial engagement had broken up? But she dismissed that possibility quickly. George would go to any lengths to spare himself 'embarrassment.'

Still, she didn't imagine it would be a comfortable few days ahead, and on that point she was right. She watched the islands disappear into tiny specks in the sea that afternoon and knew as she watched them that her last chance for love was also disappearing. She arrived at her parents' home that night with her heart aching, and when she stumbled into her mother's arms and burst into tears, her mother thought it was because of George.

'There, there now, dear,' she comforted, 'George told us all about it. I'm sure it's for the best, if you think so, although . . .' She pushed Megan a little away, a glimmer of hope trying to force its way through the frown on her brow, 'I can't help thinking how *well* the two of you always got along. Are you sure this isn't just some lovers' quarrel that can be patched up?'

Megan simply couldn't explain it to her mother that night. She pleaded a headache and went to bed.

But the next morning she began her speech, which would be repeated over and over the next few days. 'George and I were thinking about marriage for all the wrong reasons,' she said. 'There are more important things to life than financial security and a middle-class life style. We simply didn't love each other. It would have been a disaster.' And she added to her mother, 'I'm just sorry it took so long for us to discover it.'

A few days later her mother told her, 'I understand George has got rid of the house. He didn't lose a cent. His mother tells me he's decided to take an apartment in Baltimore.' She sighed. 'Such a shame! It was a gorgeous house.'

Megan could tell the time was not right for her to carry through her own plans about moving to Baltimore. Everyone would think she had simply followed George. It was a ridiculous notion, of course, because Baltimore held many attractions besides one rejected suitor, but that was the way people in small towns thought.

By the time Megan went back to work everyone in town had heard the news. She received sympathetic motions from her co-workers, but she put them off by presenting them with the souvenirs she had brought from the island. Dr Brandon was pleased that she had remembered him, and the girls were thrilled with their shell jewellery. Everyone exclaimed over her gorgeous tan.

She picked up the daily routine with an effort. She got up at seven, had breakfast with her parents, and went to work. She balanced the doctor's frantic schedule, made appointments, answered phones, made tactful requests for payment and served as intermediary between the doctor and the most persistently demanding patients. She went home, she helped her mother with the housework and dinner, and usually she went to bed before ten. Everything was the same, nothing had changed . . . except Megan.

She was not the same girl who had taken a two-week vacation for the purpose of changing her life. She had changed, but not in the way she had imagined. She had returned older, wiser, and with the sobriety only a great pain can bring. She no longer felt she belonged here—not when her heart was somewhere in the Caribbean seas with Marc Campion—but, strangely, she no longer chafed so much against the restrictions of her tightly circumscribed life. She had discovered patience. She found herself better able to bear the hectic pace of the office and the myriad irritants that assailed her. She was no longer quite so quick to argue with her mother or disagree with her father. After the pain of losing Marc, all these other little annoyances which used to have such a great importance in her life seemed pale.

Perhaps she had simply grown up.

She had one particularly close friend in the office. Sally and she usually went out to lunch together, they shared all their problems and kept no secrets. As they slid into their customary booth at the drugstore, Sally said shrewdly, 'All right, now you can tell me what *really* happened.'

Megan pretended absorption with her menu. 'What? I don't know what you're talking about.'

'Then why are you hiding behind that menu?' demanded Sally. 'You know the tuna salad is the only thing worth ordering in this place.'

Megan sighed and admitted she was right as she folded her menu. Sally told the waitress, 'The usual,' and they were left alone again. She insisted, 'So *tell* me.'

'Oh, Sally,' replied Megan morosely, 'it's so complicated! I met someone on vacation . . .'

'A man?' prompted Sally eagerly.

Megan nodded. 'He was a high-fashion photo-

grapher. He travels all over the world—a jet-setter,
so to speak.'

Sally drew in her breath appreciatively, her eyes
bright. 'Go on,' she urged.

'Oh, Sally,' Megan sighed, 'he was so wonderful—so totally different from anyone I've ever
known. He was British—not really British, but from
New Zealand, and he had the accent—but he was
so charming.'

'And good-looking?' prompted Sally.

'Oh, yes,' said Megan softly. 'But it was more
than that. We spent every day together, and he
made every day seem like a new adventure. He was
thoughtful and considerate and kind . . .'

'And you fell in love,' Sally said wonderingly.

Megan nodded. 'Almost at first sight.'

'So what happened?' insisted Sally.

Megan dropped her eyes. 'He didn't love me
back,' she said.

'Oh, Megan!' Her friend's voice was full of
sympathy. 'And that's why you broke it off with
George?'

She nodded. 'One of the reasons. I just couldn't
imagine myself living with George—and loving
Marc.'

'Oh, Megan,' said Sally sympathetically,
'couldn't you have *made* him love you? I mean,
couldn't you have arranged to see him again, or
something?'

Megan hesitated. 'What would be the point? It
would have to end sooner or later. I mean, a man
like him and a girl like me . . . it just wouldn't
work.'

Sally hesitated. 'Well,' she admitted, 'maybe it

wouldn't have ended in marriage—not everything does. But at least you would have had him for a little while.'

Yes, thought Megan, even a little while would have been better than nothing. She could have lived off the memories for ever. 'He didn't ask me,' she answered simply.

That night she unwrapped the Easter lily from its protective tissue, and the sweet fragrance that clung to it transported her immediately back to the endless white field as she lay in Marc's arms. It was another world ago, another lifetime ago, and somehow she had to find the strength to make herself believe that it was over . . .

She went to work, she came home, she gradually fell back into the old routine. The brief shining days and moonlit nights in Bermuda seemed very far away, but the memory of Marc was closer than ever.

Then one night the telephone rang, and it was George. 'I just wanted to tell you,' he said, 'that there are no hard feelings—about what happened.'

'Oh, George,' said Megan softly, 'I'm glad!'

He hesitated. 'I—er guess you heard I sold the house.'

'Yes, I did. I'm glad you didn't have to take a loss.'

'Oh, no problem there. I might have even been able to make a little profit if I'd held on to it a while longer, but I didn't want to take the chance, you know.'

'Yes,' she agreed.

Silence fell.

George said abruptly, 'Megan, I've found another girl.'

She was startled. She said, cautiously, 'Oh?'

'I hope you don't think it's too soon, after ... I mean, that I'm disloyal or anything.'

'No,' she answered quickly, 'Of course not.'

'I just didn't want you to hear it from someone else. I'm bringing her home to meet the folks this weekend.'

Megan smiled. 'I'm happy for you, George,' she said. And she really was.

He seemed relieved. 'You're a great girl, Megan.'

'Have a good life, George,' she said.

Then one morning as she was straightening the doctor's reception room, she happened to glance at the cover of a fashion magazine. Something about the clear blue water in the background and the elegant model in the foreground reminded her of Bermuda, and she picked it up, flipping through it idly. Then she caught her breath. It *was* Bermuda. There was no mistaking the fantastically shaped pillars of stone, the crystal white sand, even the hotel in one background ... She looked at the credit line. 'Photographs by Marc Campion,' and thought her heart would break.

Anxiously she looked through the magazine, examining each page now, feasting on the familiar scenery and the memory of the hand she loved which had held the camera ... She almost expected to see a picture of herself, but the section was devoted exclusively to the collection of designer swimwear. Then she remembered Marc saying, 'I keep my sweetest treasures to myself.'

Would he, she wondered, keep her photographs? Would he take them out one day, perhaps years

from now, and look through them, and would a
small smile cross his face as he remembered a
foolish young girl who had fallen in love with him
one breathless summer week on the island of
Bermuda?

Megan started to take the magazine home, to
keep it for her secret times, when she could take it
out, late at night, and be close to him by being
close to his work, to remember and relive the time
they had spent together . . . But no, she could not
start that. If she looked, she would probably see
the credit line, 'Photograph by Marc Campion'
thousands of times in her lifetime. She could not
turn into one of those crazy old ladies, clipping
keepsakes from magazines and living off of
memories from the past. She had to get her life
together again.

And then one day she came home from work
and put that possibility behind her for ever.

There was a strange black car in the driveway. It
was sleek and shiny and looked very expensive. A
car like that simply couldn't pass through Apple
Corners unremarked. She walked around it
curiously, and noticed that it had Baltimore plates
on it. The only person she really knew in
Baltimore was George, and what in the world
would George be doing driving a car like that?

She came into the house, slamming the door
behind her as she always did to announce her
arrival, and called, 'Hey, Mom, whose car is
that——'

Her mother came hurrying from the kitchen.
'Ssh!' she warned her. 'We have company!'

Megan glanced in confusion towards the living

room, where she could hear her father talking with someone. 'But who——'

At first Megan had thought her mother's high colour was simply from the heat of the oven, now she saw a bright excitement in her eyes as she caught her arm and pushed her towards the stairs. 'You'll find out soon enough,' she told her. 'Run upstairs and wash your face and change your dress—how in the world can you get so dirty sitting at a desk all day?'

There had been an accident with the mimeograph machine, and one of the children had spilled half a can of Coke on her towards the end of the day.

'Put on something pretty,' her mother advised. 'He's staying for dinner.'

'Oh, Mom!' complained Megan. 'If Daddy's going to be discussing business all night, do I really have to come down? Couldn't I just take a sandwich up to my room? It's really been a rough day . . .'

'Of *course* you have to come down!' her mother insisted, giving her a little push. 'Now don't dawdle.'

Resignedly, Megan trudged up the stairs.

As she looked through her closet she realised guiltily that she had not helped her mother with the laundry the day before as she had promised, and her wardrobe was getting a little sparse. There was a sundress she had outgrown years ago, a skirt that was too short, and a knitted dress that was missing two buttons which she had never got around to replacing. And the white dress that Marc had given her.

She had not thought to wear it again. Even looking at it brought back painful memories. But, she determined, hardening her heart, it was time to get over all that foolishness. Besides, she did not really have a choice.

She slipped on the dress and brushed her hair, reapplying a light touch of make-up before she went down to greet her father's guest. Although she knew she was a trifle overdressed for a quiet dinner at home, it would please her father to see her looking pretty and festive in the middle of the week.

As she paused at the bottom of the stairs, she heard her father call, 'Megan, is that you?'

She started towards the living room. 'Yes, Daddy.'

'Come in and see who's here!'

She paused at the door of the living room, and caught her breath. For one moment she actually felt dizzy.

For there, rising from her very own living room sofa and coming easily towards her was Marc Campion.

CHAPTER TEN

HE was dressed conservatively in a dark suit and pin-striped tie; though his eyes glinted for a moment with amusement at Megan's expression, he quickly composed his features into sobriety again as he came over to her and properly shook her hand. He looked very conservative and very successful—probably, Megan thought, for her father's benefit.

'Hello, Megan,' he said, and the rich deep timbre of his voice sent a renewed chill down her spine. 'You're looking very well.'

'M-Marc,' she whispered. She still felt weak. She could not believe what her eyes were seeing.

'Won't you come and sit down?' Marc offered politely, and Megan was aware that her father was watching her sharply.

She obeyed numbly, even though her mind was burning with a hundred questions, and she kept having to glance at him to reassure herself that she was not really imagining it. 'Mr Campion was telling me that you're quite photogenic,' her father was saying.

'Marc, please,' corrected Marc as he sat beside Megan on the sofa. 'And,' he told her, perfectly deadpan, 'I've been learning some truly fascinating things about the electronics business.'

Megan's father was the supervisor at a small

electronics firm out on the highway, and he inevitably made the mistake of assuming that everyone was as enamoured of the business as he was.

'Why didn't you tell us you'd taken on a second job while you were on vacation, Megan?' her father asked.

'It—it hardly seemed worth mentioning,' Megan explained dazedly. Then she glanced at Marc. 'I saw the feature you did on Bermuda the other day.'

'I hope you weren't too disappointed that I couldn't use you in it,' he replied soberly.

'I can't get over the fact,' put in Megan's father, 'that you actually get paid for taking pictures of pretty girls!'

'Oh, yes,' agreed Marc, 'and quite well, too, if I may say so. Although fashion photography is not my only speciality. I've also done photographic reporting in such places as Zaire and the Middle East. Although I find hard journalism much more rewarding, the fashion industry, alas, offers much higher fees.'

That would impress her father, thought Megan. While he might glance askance at a man who made his living taking pictures of girls in swimsuits, he could only admire someone who risked his life in the hot spots of the world for the principle of a free press. And best of all, Marc had put it in such as way as to paint himself as just another working-class man, never hinting at the fact that he could buy and sell a dozen men like her father if he chose.

'Now that sounds exciting,' agreed Megan's

father. 'I suppose you're too young to have seen any real action?'

'As a matter of fact,' began Marc, leaning forward a little as though to embark on a long, hair-raising tale, 'I was in Cambodia in 'seventy-one . . .'

Megan murmured, 'Excuse me—I have to help Mother with dinner.'

Marc rose politely, and Megan heard her father insisting, 'Go on,' as she hurried from the room.

She leaned agained the dining room door, breathless, touching her hot cheeks wonderingly. She felt like Alice Through the Looking Glass. What *was* going on? What was Marc doing here, having dinner with her family, making such a concentrated effort to impress her father and not doing a half bad job of it either, she had to admit. How had he found her? *Why?*

Her mother came in through the swinging door from the kitchen just then, a bowl of vegetables in her hands. 'Oh, Megan,' she said, 'I'm glad you're here. Help me get everything on the table before it gets cold.' Then she looked up and smiled at her daughter. 'Are you surprised?'

'Y-yes,' she managed.

'Oh, darling,' said her mother, 'you didn't mention a word!' She walked over and hugged her daughter swiftly. 'Well, *I* think he's perfectly charming!' she told her. 'So polite, and well-groomed, and he seems *very* responsible to me. Now your father may take a little longer, but that's only because you'll always be his baby girl. You just remember you're over twenty-one and you make your own decision.'

Megan stared at her. She did not understand at all.

Her mother served fried chicken and spoon bread and fresh vegetables and baked apples, and Marc raved over the meal. Already, Megan could tell in some amusement, he had found his way into her mother's heart. 'I spend so much time eating hotel food,' he confessed, 'a meal like this is pure ambrosia.'

'Hotel food is bad for the digestion,' agreed Megan's father. 'You should settle down and get a house of your own.'

'Of course I'd like nothing better,' agreed Marc, 'but the problems of finding a good housekeeper have hardly seemed worth the rewards, as I am so seldom in one place long enough to call it home.'

'You need,' suggested her mother, 'a wife.' And she added innocuously, 'Megan's an excellent cook.'

Megan stared at her, horrified. But Marc only replied easily, with a warm smile at Megan, 'If she's inherited only half your talent, then your daughter is twice blessed.'

Even though Megan intended to have some stern words with her mother on the subject of matchmaking, Marc had managed to rescue the awkward moment with his usual savoire-faire.

When dinner was finished, Megan's father rose and said to Marc, 'You were telling me about your assignment in Iran. Let's go in the den where we can——'

'Carl,' interrupted her mother meaningfully, 'don't you think you and Marc could continue your conversation another time? I could use some help with the dishes, and,' she suggested as her husband seemed to be slow to understand, 'Megan and Marc might like some time to talk—alone.'

Although he did not seem at all pleased with this turn of events, Megan's father rather uncharitably agreed, and began to clear the table. Marc smiled at Megan as he held open the door to the living room for her.

Once through it, he closed the door behind him and turned to her, a deep light of passion sparking in his eyes as he slipped his arms about her. 'Now,' he said huskily, 'let's begin this evening in the proper fashion.'

He swept her close to him and kissed her hungrily, his lips burning their demand into hers as she grew weak with the emotions that washed over her—the hot electric thrill only being in his presence automatically generated, the breathless dizziness that assaulted her as his kiss drew her into the heights of ecstasy. She wrapped her arms about his neck and a little cry escaped her as she entangled her fingers in the silkiness of his hair and felt the hard muscles of his neck beneath her hands.

'Darling,' he whispered at last, looking down at her with an eager hunger in his eyes, 'you look beautiful. When I saw you in that dress it was all I could do to keep from sweeping you into my arms, your father notwithstanding.'

'Oh, Marc,' she replied tremulously, 'I—I don't

understand . . . What are you doing here? How did you find me?'

He smiled and clasped both her hands, drawing her over to the sofa. 'It wasn't a task demanding great astuteness,' he returned lightly. 'I simply had Gayle call every Brown in Apple Corners until he found a family with a daughter named Megan.'

They sat down on the sofa, her hands still clasped tightly in his, and she searched his face joyfully, expectantly, but with some confusion. Although the only thing that really mattered now was that he was here, beside her once more, and that he had come for her—actually sought her out—she could not contain her curiosity. 'But—but *why*? I thought—I thought you never wanted to see me again . . .'

'What a foolish notion!' he exclaimed. Then, gently, he traced the outline of her jaw with his forefinger, his eyes probing deep into hers. 'My sweet little poppet,' he said softly, 'did you really imagine I'd just let you disappear from my life like that?'

Her joy seemed to be choking her. She was in his arms again, lost in the wonder of his mouth upon hers, then lying back against the cushions as his lips traced a burning pattern on her neck and her breasts and his fingers lightly stroked her abdomen through the thin material. 'Darling, I want you,' he whispered. 'I couldn't get you out of my mind no matter how hard I tried, you haunted me day and night . . . Megan, oh, my dear, my very dear, Megan . . .'

His mouth covered hers again, and a joy like

none she had every known coursed through her, setting her veins on fire and turning her limbs to water. He wanted her ... he had come for her ...

And then he lifted himself a little, holding her face between both his hands, looking into her eyes eagerly. 'Darling,' he insisted, 'let me be the one. Let me teach you. I can show you the world— London, Paris, Rome ... Tokyo, Venice, Amsterdam ... We'll explore the Emperor's gardens together, the Pharaohs' tombs, we'll cross the desert on camels and track a Bengal tiger in the heart of India ... you'll never lack for adventure, my angel, as long as you're with me ... And I'll show you love.' The thick velvety lashes slowly hid the fire in his eyes as he brought his lips once again to hers.

Passion built slowly as he explored her lips deliberately, sensuously, holding her face gently between his hands as he unfolded for her a hint of the wonders that were yet to come. Then he groaned softly and pulled her to a sitting position, though still holding her firmly against the sturdy beating of his heart. 'What a fool you make of me,' he said deeply. 'In another moment that door will open, and this is *not* the way to make a good impression on your father!'

The very thought had the power to subdue Megan's passion for the moment, although her cheeks were still hot and her breath was not coming with its usual regularity when Marc pushed her away a moment later, smiling down at her.

'I told your parents,' he said, 'that I wanted to

employ you as a full time model. *That*'s my excuse for being here.'

She looked at him for a moment longer, breathlessly, then dropped her eyes. She had to do something to break the wonderful tension that was building within her before she simply exploded with joy. 'I don't know whether I'll accept your offer,' she replied demurely, teasing him. 'After all, you never paid me for the last time.'

He lifted her chin with his finger, and the corners of his eyes crinkled with his smile. 'The pay might not be much,' he agreed, 'but the fringe benefits are simply spectacular . . . gowns from all the best houses in Paris, cruises and parties with the smart set, and unlimited credit with your employer . . . are you tempted?'

Now Megan understood what her mother had meant when she had said, 'You're over twenty-one . . . make your own decision.' But she had to ask, 'What you told my parents . . . do you really want me to model for you?'

'No,' he answered, and his voice and his expression was serious. 'That was only a way to get my foot in the door. I'm not asking you to model for me, Megan; although I expect to photograph you often, it will be purely for my own pleasure, and not for commercial gain. I'm too selfish to share you with the world.'

She dropped her eyes, but, with a gentle pressure of his finger, Marc forced her to look at him again. His eyes were a very deep blue. 'Do you mind?' he asked.

She whispered, 'No.'

'Megan . . .' his voice was very sober, 'do you

understand quite clearly what I'm asking?'

She nodded. He was asking her to be his mistress.

'And your answer?'

She searched his eyes with a depth of love and wanting that could not be mistaken. 'You know I only want to be with you,' she whispered.

She saw the flame of passion leap into his eyes, but he contented himself with merely kissing both of her hands violently and quickly. 'And now,' he said softly, 'I think I must leave you, while I'm still able.'

He stood, and smiled down at her, taking out his handkerchief. 'I'll go say goodnight to your parents. Were you wearing lipstick, or did I kiss it all off?'

'No,' she answered, standing beside him. 'I wasn't wearing any.'

He looked at her for a moment longer, his eyes lingering on her lips, before he replaced his handkerchief. 'Of course,' he said softly, 'the only woman I know who can look as devastating without make-up as with it.'

He turned to go back towards the kitchen. 'I'll see you tomorrow, and we'll make our plans,' he promised.

Megan went to work the next day in a daze, trying hard to convince herself she had not simply dreamed the entire thing. But she knew it was not a dream when she came home and found Marc just leaving her front door.

'Hello, love,' he said softly as she came near and they met on the steps. His eyes were deep with the light of appreciation and welcome. He took her arm. 'Let's go for a walk. We have a lot to talk about, and not much time to do it in, I'm afraid. I have to be back in New York tomorrow.'

She looked at him in despair. 'Oh, Marc, you're not leaving! Not so soon!'

He smiled at her. 'You'd do well to hide your impatience, poppet,' he retorted. 'We'll only be separated for a few days, if all goes well. And I do have quite a few details to wind up before we embark on that extended world tour we talked about last night.'

She drew in her breath, her eyes shining, all else momentarily forgotten. 'Do you mean it? Are we really going to all those places?'

He slipped an arm about her shoulders and squeezed them briefly. 'All that and more. You have far too many gaps in your education, lovey, and a trip around the world will begin to fill in some of them nicely. The others, of course . . .' he looked at her deeply and with a meaning that sent a rush of blood to Megan's cheeks, 'I'll take care of personally.'

He dropped his arm to a more impersonal touch on her elbow as they walked along the street, shady with elms in the lazy summer heat and bright with flower beds. 'Now,' he continued briskly, 'I've spent the entire day with your parents—with your father at his office, and your mother here at home, trying to convince them that you'll be quite safe with me . . .'

She looked at him. 'I'll bet you succeeded, too!'

Marc Campion could convince anyone of anything he wanted to.

He replied seriously, 'I couldn't have it on my conscience that they were worrying unnecessarily, so I did my best. Of course it's not easy for them, love, so you must be patient.'

Megan felt a rush of love for him. She knew he would never hint to her parents what his *real* interest in their daughter was, and though she felt miserably guilty about this, she was a grown-up woman and capable of making her own decisions. She had never before deceived them, but it was only to spare their feelings that they must embark on this charade, and she was grateful for Marc's sensitivity.

'As I said,' he went on, 'I must be off in the morning, so let me tell you what I want you to do. Your passport is in order, I take it? Of course you'll have to get visas, but I'll arrange all that for you in New York. On the first leg of our journey we'll visit only the Western countries, so we won't have to bother about nasty things like shots for a time. Since we'd have to make a connecting flight in New York anyway, what I suggest is this: You make all your arrangements here, say your goodbyes, cancel your magazine subscriptions, etcetera ...' his eyes twinkled at her, 'and then join me in New York on the seventeenth. We can leave together on the eighteenth—unless you'd like to spend some time exploring New York?'

Megan was dazed. That was a little over a week away! It was all happening so fast. 'N-no,' she managed to reply in a moment, 'the eighteenth will be fine.'

He glanced at her. 'Not having second thoughts, are you?'

'N-no, it's just that . . .' she spread her hands helplessly, 'it's so soon! There's so much to do!'

'One thing I insist upon,' Marc told her. 'Don't go bringing along a mountain of luggage. Pack only what you absolutely need, because I intend to refurbish your wardrobe entirely from every continental city we visit. There shouldn't be that much to do,' he added. 'Just throw some things into a suitcase and say goodbye.'

She laughed helplessly. She supposed, to a widely-travelled man like himself, it must seem that way.

'I'll call you from New York,' he promised as they circled the block and reached his car again, 'and let you know about your flight.' He kissed her tenderly on the cheek. 'I'll miss you, darling, but in only a few days we need never be separated again!'

But something about that statement made Megan a little uneasy. Of course she was happier than she had ever been in her life, just knowing she would be with him, but it was not exactly permanent . . . He had made no promises to her. He had never even said he loved her.

She remembered with a small, bitter smile her foolish ideas of what a 'modern' relationship meant. She had thought it would be so easy, in her childlike view of the world, but the reality was quite different. The reality tinged with insecurity and doubt which she must be strong enough to overcome. The reality meant desperately loving a man who might never make a commitment to her, and trying not to see herself growing old and alone. Marc had offered her exactly the type of open, noncommittal relationship she had thought she wanted ... but was it enough?

It would have to be, she decided, though not without a small pang of regret. If this was all he offered, then it would have to be enough, because she loved him too much to think otherwise. Her ideas of liberation and sophistication no longer seemed to enter into the picture, for all that mattered was that she would be with the man she loved, in any circumstances.

She tried to push aside the doubts that threatened to spoil her happiness in the furiously busy days ahead. It didn't matter, it really didn't, because she had all she wanted and couldn't ask for more. She had Marc, the man she loved, she had a life filled with adventure by his side awaiting her, and this was the twentieth century; she did not need a promise of marriage to make her life complete.

She knew her father did not want her to go, but he was very careful not to let his misgivings show. He only asked once, 'Are you very sure this is what you want, Megan?'

She assured him genuinely that it was, but then she had to leave him quickly, remembering that he thought she was only going off to pursue a new and exciting career, not to live without the inconveniences of marriage with the man she loved.

Her mother was more enthusiastic, for, being female, she had completely fallen victim to Marc's incorrigible charm. She helped Megan choose carefully the few items from her wardrobe she would need, and made arrangements for the remainder of her things to be packed away. She never shed a tear. In fact, she seemed more enthusiastic about the adventure that was unfolding before her daughter than Megan did herself. 'I can't believe you're taking this all so calmly,' her mother exclaimed. 'Why, if it were me, I'd be at my wits' end!'

Megan realised she was rather subdued, and although she knew the reason why, she could not tell her mother. 'I guess I'm a little numb,' she answered. 'It's an awfully big step.'

And then her mother looked at her. 'Megan,' she said, 'you *do* love him, don't you?'

Megan stared at her mother. She remembered Marc's saying sagely, 'Mothers always know.' So it had shown in her eyes! She hesitated, uncertain whether her mother would still approve of the venture if she knew how desperately in love Megan was with her potential 'employer', but she could not lie to her. 'Yes,' she admitted, 'I do.'

Her mother hugged her. 'Then you should be happy! Get that worried look off your face— darling, your life is just beginning!'

Of course, everyone was very impressed that plain little Megan Brown was going off with an internationally famous photographer to be a fashion model, and a 'home town girl makes good' atmosphere pervaded the entire community. The girls at the office gave her a going-away party, and it was hard for Megan to stop the sentimental tears. Of course she had everything she had ever wanted, excitement, adventure, romance . . . But it wasn't easy to say goodbye to her familiar environment in favour of the uncertain new life that awaited her.

'I can't believe how lucky you are,' exclaimed Sally, her eyes sparkling. 'It's like a fairy-tale come true!'

'Yes,' agreed Megan, trying to muster the same enthusiasm she saw in her friend's face, 'it is.'

'I mean,' Sally went on, 'maybe it's not for ever, but at least now you have a *chance*.'

Megan tried to laugh away her nervousness. 'I guess you're right I just can't believe it's all happening. I mean, I just—I'm just not the kind of girl things like this happen to!'

And deep down, Megan knew she was not that kind of girl at all. She also knew that men like Marc Campion hardly ever married their mistresses. What would happen when she got old, or he got tired of her? She wondered in despair whether the bitter, vengeful Olivette had started out this way.

She tried to put all those depressing thoughts behind her as she said a quick goodbye to her parents at the airport. They had arrived late, and it was all too hasty and casual—as though she was only going away on a short trip. She knew that it might be years before she saw her parents again, and when she did she would no longer be the innocent, demure daughter they had loved and protected for twenty-three years. She managed not to cry until she was on board, and then she looked out the window and let the tears stream down her cheeks, and she knew that if the plane were not beginning to taxi down the runway she would have got off and run back to the safety of the familiar.

But then she was disembarking in the huge, busy airport in New York City, and Marc was hurrying towards her. He crushed her against him, and she was so safe and happy to be in his arms again that nothing else seemed very important. 'What was that sad little expression on your face I saw a minute ago?' he demanded as he began to lead her through the crowd. 'You looked as if you were about to face an executioner!'

She laughed a little. 'Just sentiment, I guess! It's all happening so fast and I . . .' she faltered, 'I've never done anything like this before.'

His eyes were warm as he smiled at her. 'Don't go getting homesick on me,' he warned. 'At least, not on our first day abroad!'

Megan smiled gaily and assured him she would not. And if she did, she told herself silently, she would make certain he never guessed it.

Her flight had arrived late in the afternoon, and Marc had her luggage sent ahead to the hotel while they did a quick tour of the city. Then he took her to dinner in one of New York's most elegant restaurants, and by the time they finally went back to the hotel Megan was dizzy with excitement and the whirlwind pace her life had suddenly taken, which seemed to have culminated with this day.

But, as he escorted her down the plushly

carpeted hotel corridor, she suddenly realised that
the adventure had only begun. This would be their
night, their first night together . . . Her heart began
to pound dryly in her throat as Marc unlocked the
door and led her inside the room.

At first she was confused, for although she looked
around the room for signs of his occupancy, the only
luggage she saw was her own. And then she ventured
hesitantly, 'Separate rooms?'

He smiled, and took her shoulders, turning her
around to face him gently. 'I know this is all rather
sudden for you, Megan,' he said. 'I thought you
might like some privacy on your first night. You
must be tired, and you need some time alone to
relax.'

She felt an enormous gratitude swell within her,
and to her confusion, relief. Then he bent down
and kissed her lightly, then drew her to him
tightly, embracing her with his cheek resting
against her hair. 'Darling,' he said huskily, 'I *do*
want you, and my impatience is such that it was
hard for me to bring you here tonight, instead of
my own room, which is just across the hall . . . But
I want the first time to be special for you, magical
and memorable, not just a night together snatched
between flights.'

He lifted her face and kissed her lips again
briefly. She could feel the restrained passion in his
touch, and see the tension in his eyes. Then he
whispered, 'Sleep well, love,' and left her.

They went to the airport early the next
morning and had breakfast in the restaurant
overlooking the busy concourse. Megan could
feel her eagerness and her excitement building.

She still could not quite convince herself she was not dreaming. 'Where will we go first?' she demanded, her eyes bright. 'You haven't even told me!'

'How does Paris sound?' Marc suggested, his own eyes reflecting back the sparkle in hers. 'Champagne and strawberries for breakfast every morning!'

She laughed, and reached across the table for his hand. His strong brown fingers squeezed hers joyfully, and the thrill that bubbled through her eyes at so simple a thing as his touch was childlike and irresistible.

'Ah,' he exclaimed softly, 'How I shall love seeing the world through your eyes! The Champs Elysées, the river Seine, the sidewalk cafés, the chateaux of the Loire . . . would you like to stay in one of those chateaux, my love? For a week, or a month, or until you grow bored?'

Her eyes widened. 'Oh, Marc, could we? Oh, I——' And suddenly she stopped, her expression frozen, her eyes fixed on something beyond his shoulder.

'Marc!' she cried, and began to fumble with her bag, starting to rise. 'It's my parents! I saw them!'

Marc turned in his seat, and he saw them, too, although they were now moving down the concourse in the opposite direction. 'So it is,' he commented, and turned back to her.

'They've come to see me off,' she explained frantically, 'all this way . . .' So *that* was why the goodbyes in Baltimore had been so brief and casual! They must have planned a weekend in New

York to surprise her by seeing her off at the airport!

'Sit down, poppet,' Marc suggested, catching her hand. 'Finish your coffee.'

'But they've come all this way—just to say goodbye—if I don't hurry I'll lose them, and it would be terrible to miss each other at the last minute in this crowd! I've got to see them!'

He pulled firmly at her hand. 'You'll have plenty of time to see them,' he told her, sipping his tea, 'on the plane.'

Megan sat down abruptly. At first she thought she must have misunderstood. 'The—the plane?' she repeated. 'What on earth are you talking about, Marc? My parents——'

'Wouldn't dream of missing their only daughter's wedding,' he replied calmly.

She could say nothing for a long time. She simply stared at him. And then she said, not blinking, hardly even breathing, in a very weak voice, 'Wedding?'

'Well, it is customary, isn't it,' he demanded, 'to have a wedding before embarking on a honeymoon?'

'H-honeymoon?'

'Darling, *will* you stop repeating everything I say?' he requested impatiently. 'Now, if you'd only give me a chance, I was about to outline our itinerary for you. First, we're bound for New Zealand——'

'New *Zealand*?'

He gave an exasperated sigh. 'There you go again! Would you like to tell this, or may I?'

Megan fell silent, but it was only because she

was too numb to think of anything to say.

'My parents are much older than yours,' he told her, 'and very set in their ways. It would break their hearts if I weren't married in the same parish church in which they've worshipped all their lives. I felt it would be easier for your parents to make the trip to my home town.'

With a great effort, she restrained herself from parroting his last words. 'Do-o you mean, my parents—are going to *New Zealand*? With *us*?'

Marc grinned. 'It wasn't easy to convince them, I assure you, but as you can see, here they are. My silver tongue saved me one last time. I asked them to keep it secret,' he confided. 'I wanted it to be a surprise for you.'

Slowly it began to sink in. Marriage! He was asking her to marry him, to live with him for ever and be his wife . . . 'But,' she exclaimed, 'you must have told them from the beginning that this was what you intended to do! No wonder they let me go so easily—they knew I was getting married!'

'Darling,' he explained patiently, 'I may be gifted, but I'm no fool. It was hard enough to convince your father to approve of your marrying a foreigner whom he had never met and allowing her to go traipsing all over the world with said stranger, much less . . .' He broke off with a self-explanatory shrug.

She looked at him, warmth and love building up within her until tears sparkled in her eyes. Yet he had let her think she was going off with him into some casual living arrangement, the epitome of the modern girl . . . his final object lesson.

He reached forward and stroked her eyelid

lightly with his finger, tenderness and love in his eyes. 'My precious poppet,' he said softly, 'you know I adore you. Why the tears?'

Megan blinked them away rapidly and clasped his hand, holding it for a moment against her cheek. 'I'm just so happy!' she whispered.

Marc brought her fingers to his lips and kissed them gently, then brought their entwined hands to rest on the table. 'Now,' he said enthusiastically, 'to continue with our itinerary. After a week or two at home, while we all get to know one another's families, there'll be a fine wedding— white gown, of course . . .' he inserted with a twinkle. 'And then we'll begin our honeymoon. It will be the longest honeymoon in history,' he assured her, 'beginning in Paris, of course, and not ending until we've seen every major attraction the world has to offer. We'll take a year, or maybe two, for our tour—cruises to the Greek Islands, rickshaws in China, gondolas in Venice—and after that, we'll return home to set up house. I'm not quite sure where, yet, but it will be a small town— perhaps near Baltimore?—with plenty of parks and playgrounds and good schools, because by that time, of course, you'll be pregnant with the first of our two-point-two children . . .'

Megan laughed, helpless with joy and delighted by the perfectly serious tone of his speech. Marc's eyes twinkled and he gave her an endearing grin. 'You may be a liberated woman, Megan Brown,' he told her, 'but you're about to marry a very old-fashioned boy!'

For a moment longer she only sat there, basking in the love that radiated from his eyes, feeling her own love growing and building into something that would last for ever. Then their flight was called and they quickly gathered up their things and left the restaurant. In the concourse, Marc paused and kissed her once, lingeringly, then he slipped his arm around her, hurrying her towards a future bright with promise.

A WORD ABOUT THE AUTHOR

Rebecca Flanders is a professional romance author with the ability to write love stories to suit all sorts of different tastes. Not only is she capable of creating novels for Harlequin Presents—*Morning Song* (#632) and *Falkone's Promise* (#666)—but she has already gained recognition as a Harlequin American Romance author. Her novels in that series include *Twice in a Lifetime* (free with subscription), *A Matter of Trust* (#6), *Best of Friends* (#24) and *Suddenly Love* (#41).

Such success, however, was not something that Rebecca achieved overnight. Although she completed her first novel when she was nineteen, it never reached publication — nor did dozens of other attempts during the next few years. Yet these were valuable years for, as the author states, "I spent every spare moment perfecting my skills...until I sold my first novel in 1979."

She was born and raised in the state of Georgia, where she currently lives. She enjoys oil and watercolor painting, music—listening and composing—but, she says, with writing and her eleven-year-old daughter keeping her busy, "who has time for hobbies?"

Coming Next Month in Harlequin Romance!

2629 A GIRL CALLED ANDY   Rosemary Badger
A tempestuous romance about a young teacher trying to
forge a life for herself and her younger siblings in
Tasmania—without the interference of her autocratic
neighbor, a handsome novelist.

2630 MAELSTROM   Ann Cooper
An arrogant oil executive believes that Samantha, a British
engineer, has no place in Saudi Arabia—except perhaps in
his bed! Samantha tries heroically to resist his charm and
prove him wrong.

2631 THE CHEQUERED SILENCE   Jacqueline Gilbert
A young actress deserts her man—a famous director—for
reasons she fears to divulge. When they meet again years
later, he still cannot forgive her—nor can she reveal her
secret....

2632 DESERT FLOWER   Dana James
Two British doctors, one an opinionated male and the other
a beautiful woman, fight for their different points of view—
and fight against their mutual attraction—in an Egyptian
oasis clinic.

2633 ONCE MORE WITH FEELING   Natalie Spark
Life becomes unbearably complicated for a young English
actress when she performs in a play directed by her one-time
idol, a man who years before humiliated her—and betrayed
her actress mother!

2634 ALMOST A STRANGER   Margaret Way
Sydney, Australia, is the setting for this intriguing love story
of a young woman caught in a family feud—and caught in
the throes of desire for a man she finds just too disturbing....

Harlequin Photo Calendar

Turn Your Favorite Photo into a Calendar.

JULY 1984

The Browns

Uniquely yours, this 10x17½" calendar features your favorite photograph, with any name you wish in attractive lettering at the bottom. A delightfully personal and practical idea!

Send us your favorite color print, black-and-white print, negative, or slide, any size (we'll return it), along with **3** proofs of purchase (coupon below) from a June or July release of Harlequin Romance, Harlequin Presents, Harlequin Superromance, Harlequin American Romance or Harlequin Temptation, plus $5.75 (includes shipping and handling).

Harlequin Celebrates

Thirty-five Years of Excellence

...and our commitment to excellence continues. Indulge in the pleasure of superb romance reading by choosing the most popular love stories in the world.

Harlequin Presents

Exciting romance novels for the woman of today— a rare blend of passion and dramatic realism.

Harlequin Romance ™

Tender, captivating stories that sweep to faraway places and delight with the magic of love.

HARLEQUIN SUPERROMANCE ™

Longer, more absorbing love stories for the connoisseur of romantic fiction.

Harlequin Temptation ™

Sensual and romantic stories about choices, dilemmas, resolutions, and above all, the fulfillment of love.

Harlequin American Romance ™

Contemporary romances— uniquely North American in flavor and appeal.

Code: 35-1

Share the joys and sorrows of real-life love with

Harlequin American Romance!™

Discover the new and unique

Harlequin Gothic and Regency Romance Specials!

Gothic Romance	Regency Romance
THE CASTLE AT JADE COVE	A GENTLEMAN'S AGREEMENT
Helen Hicks	Deborah Lynne
AN INNOCENT MADNESS	REVENGE FOR A DUCHESS
Dulcie Hollyock	Sara Orwig
RESTLESS OBSESSION	MIDNIGHT FOLLY
Jane Toombs	Phyllis Pianka

A new and exciting world of romance reading

Harlequin Gothic and Regency Romance Specials!